Basement Dwellers

Holly Copella

ISBN: 0-9864416-7-8
ISBN-13: 978-0-9864416-7-7

To Papa Lou

ACKNOWLEDGMENTS

Copella Books: First Paperback Edition 2015
Cover Artist: Shardel
SelfPubBookCovers.com/Shardel
Printed by CreateSpace, An Amazon.com Company

PUBLISHER'S NOTE

Chapter One

The quaint town of Emmerich, with its historic German homes and quiet streets, seemed alive with activity despite the dreary, rainy evening. Main Street was congested with cars driving through partially flooded roadways. Some drove cautiously while others refused to allow a little standing water impede their schedules. A black, stretch limousine drove cautiously through the flooded roadways, not caring about the impatient driver in the sports car behind it. The limousine driver was a neatly dressed man in his mid-forties, Brandon Davenport. He was a refined, clean-shaven man who obviously took pride in his appearance. He sat excessively straight behind the wheel and showed great care while driving the expensive limousine through the flooded roads. A casually dressed woman in her early twenties, Lexx Davenport, slouched in the passenger seat and avoided looking at her Uncle Brandon.

Beyond her simple, country girl look, she was actually quite attractive, not that she was the least bit concerned with her appearance or how others perceived her. She wore her hair carelessly tossed into a ponytail and didn't bother with makeup. She obviously didn't share her uncle's taste in fine clothing and expensive cologne. Brandon cast a look at her several times, but it was obvious she wasn't interested in their current conversation.

"I'm just asking you to consider it," Brandon suggested in a delicate tone.

She shifted uncomfortably in her seat but still refused to look at him. "Why is it every time we drive together it's the same conversation?" Lexx asked.

"You're twenty-five years old, Lexx--"

"Twenty-four."

By the look on his face, he was reluctant to believe he'd been wrong. "Close enough," he muttered and again glanced at her. "You should be dating. I worry about you."

She finally looked at him, stared into his green eyes, and grinned deviously. "Are you worried that I might turn out like you, Uncle Brandon?"

Brandon didn't hesitate before responding with, "It's crossed my mind--yes."

"I'll make you a deal," she announced with enthusiasm and finally looked at him as she straightened in her seat. "I'll start dating when you do."

Brandon glared at her. Her sly grin mocked him, and he didn't approve.

"Now you're just being plain mean," he replied and appeared uncomfortable at the suggestion.

Lexx remained playful. She'd finally called him on his own game and now it was her turn to make him squirm. "But you should be dating." Her look turned serious despite the tiny smile she attempted to hide. "I worry about you."

Brandon again glared at her. Lexx smiled and laughed at the look he gave her. She actually couldn't imagine her uncle dating, although there had been rumors that he was quite the charmer in college. To her knowledge, he hadn't dated since she was a little girl. She was sure he was terribly out of practice, although, he would make a fine catch for any woman. He was as domesticated as they came and always picked up after himself. She suddenly found herself wondering what was wrong with him that he wasn't married already.

"I'm starting to see why your parents moved to Florida," he remarked. "It's payback for the way I treated your father when we were kids."

"It could be a lot worse."

"I don't see how," he muttered while watching the road before him.

"I could be more like Carson."

Brandon stared out the rain-covered windshield and appeared deep in thought. Something clicked in his head, and he was instantly concerned.

"You're right. That would be worse." He inhaled deeply and sighed. "I love Carson, but he's--"

"A bit of a whore?"

He suddenly glared a disapproving look at her. "That's not nice," Brandon scolded sternly then became unusually silent a moment. "--but accurate."

"Look on the bright side; I'll take care of you when you're old and senile."

Her comment made him chuckle, but he was quick to wipe the smirk from his face so as not to encourage her bad behavior. "Not that I don't enjoy our weekend movie marathons, but I'm looking forward to dancing with you at your wedding and maybe holding my grandniece."

Lexx was horrified by the comment and stared at him with her mouth hanging open. "Oh, God!" she suddenly gasped with alarm. "Now you want me to pop out a few kids while I'm at it? You're a monster!"

"You're my favorite niece," he announced cheerfully while grinning.

Her eyes narrowed. "I'm your only niece."

The limousine drove through another large puddle on the congested roadway. Despite the heavy traffic, the sports car behind them sped past the limousine. Its engine sounded like a racecar, startling both. Brandon stared out the flooded windshield and shook his head at the passing car.

"Damned idiot," he scoffed and refrained from using more colorful language.

His usage of expletives only encouraged Lexx to use them more often, so he'd been cutting back. Lexx thought he showed excellent restraint considering he was behind the wheel. Her Uncle Brandon was notorious for driving under the influence of expletives. His explosive cursing outbursts were funny when she was five years old, and it was still funny nearly twenty years later.

"Someone should tell him it's raining," Brandon muttered with annoyance. He almost certainly withheld the colorful name he wanted to call the driver.

"Don't worry, Uncle Brandon," Lexx announced. "He's a twenty-something. They're invincible."

"Yeah?" he remarked and raised a curious brow. "Tell that to our passenger."

"Don't worry," she replied in a stern tone. "Roger and I are going to have a nice long talk when we get home."

Her uncle snorted a laugh and cast a sideways glance at her. "I'm sure it'll be very one-sided," Brandon announced while grinning. "If he has anything to say for himself, you'll be sure to let me know, right?"

She was humored by the comment and muttered lowly, "You'll be the first to know."

The sports car got stuck behind a brand new Buick just a few cars ahead of the limousine and impatiently rode the car's rear end, looking for any opportunity to pass. Within the Buick, a couple in their early thirties watched the road ahead with deep puddles of standing water. The man behind the wheel, Eric Martin, suddenly appeared more interested in the car riding his bumper. His wife, Ava Martin, sat in the passenger seat alongside him and alternated watching the road and looking at a pamphlet in her hand.

"It says here they have a spa," Ava informed her husband enthusiastically then looked at him and grinned. "A couple's massage sounds romantic."

He chuckled softly while alternating watching the road and the sports car behind him. "I don't understand a woman's idea of romantic," he replied. "What's romantic about another woman giving your husband a massage?" His teasing grin mocked her. "If you want romantic, you should be the one giving me the massage. Now that sounds like fun."

She laughed and deviously raised her brows. "Oh, I see," Ava replied. "So it's anything goes this weekend?"

"Exactly," he replied. "Anything goes is every man's idea of romantic." Eric's good mood was cut short and his expression turned annoyed as he looked in the rearview mirror. "What the hell is wrong with this asshole?"

Ava felt compelled to turn in her seat and look behind them to the impatient sports car buzzing to the center looking for an opportunity to bolt past them. The sports car saw a small opening and attempted to pass the Buick despite the oncoming car several yards ahead in the left lane. The sports car suddenly hydroplaned and swerved out of control, slamming into the Buick. The Buick spun radically upon impact. Ava screamed while her husband attempted to control the car's spin. The sports car was propelled into a roll and struck the approaching car in the opposite lane.

Not far behind the disastrous scene, within the limousine, Brandon and Lexx were horrified by the chain reaction of cars crashing in front of them. Brandon hit the brakes and attempted to maneuver the limousine from the wreck now directly in front of them. Lexx screamed and clung to her car door. The limousine slid sideways to avoid the spinning Buick in front of it. It nearly cleared the spinning car when it was struck by a truck sliding out of control to avoid the rolling sports car. The limousine was thrown in the opposite direction from the direct hit to its mid-section and sent it rolling across the roadway until it struck a parked car.

The sports car was torn apart as it continued to roll out of control before crashing roof first into a garbage truck. The car was flattened nearly beyond recognition. Several other cars attempted to avoid the collision now blocking both lanes and became involved as well. The sounds of squealing tires, shattering glass, and twisting metal was deafening despite the sound of the pouring rain. Cars continued to crash into one another from both lanes leaving a massive pile-up. More than twenty vehicles were crushed together crossing the span of both lanes and along the curbs into parked cars in a massive collection of torn metal and shattered fiberglass.

Chapter Two

Lexx lie slumped against the seat as blood flowed from a laceration on her right temple. She slowly woke and appeared disoriented. She gingerly touched her bleeding temple and gasped with pain. Reality still hadn't set in. Lexx glanced around with confusion then looked at her uncle in the driver's seat and attempted to focus on him. Brandon was slumped against the wheel, despite the deflated airbag and his seatbelt, neither having done their job properly. He bled from his head and had several other visible injuries. As she stared at her uncle, Lexx felt alarm sweep through her, and reality flooded back. She frantically attempted to unbuckle her seatbelt while staring at her motionless uncle behind the wheel. From her position across the seat from where he lie slumped, it was difficult to tell if he was breathing or not.

"Uncle Brandon? Uncle Brandon!"

He didn't respond to her cries. Lexx finally released her seatbelt and slid across the seat to him. She gently touched his shoulder. He fell back against the seat without waking.

"Uncle Brandon?" she gasped with horror.

Lexx placed her fingers to his neck and felt for a pulse. Her expression suddenly shattered. Lexx turned to her door and attempted to open it, but it wouldn't give. The massive pile-up was staggering to behold as passersby ran from every corner and building to the smashed vehicles in an attempt to assist those injured and stuck within their cars. The limousine door flew open with a thunderous crack, and Lexx tumbled from the vehicle to the pavement. A man approached and attempted to help her to her feet. She pulled away from him and wasted little time leaping across the limousine's wrinkled hood. She slid across the wet, crumpled hood to the driver's side. Lexx aggressively pulled the door open and removed Brandon's seatbelt. Another passerby quickly approached as she pulled his limp body from the seat.

"No, you shouldn't move him," the passerby frantically yelled to her.

Lexx forcibly dragged Brandon from the limousine and to the pavement. Despite the size difference between them, her strength at that moment was astounding. Ambulance and police sirens were heard approaching from every direction in the near distance. Lexx dropped to her knees alongside her uncle and immediately performed CPR on him. Within seconds, a rugged looking EMT in her late twenties, Monica Burke, approached Lexx and Brandon with her medical bag. Another EMT around the same age, Evan Marshal, appeared directly behind her.

"Watch out! We've got this," Monica said and brushed Lexx aside.

Lexx scrambled away from Brandon on her backside as Monica and Evan moved in and checked for a pulse. Lexx remained kneeling near them and just stared at Brandon's lifeless body as the rain soaked them, washing his blood away in a pink stream. From Lexx's perspective, everything seemed to be moving in slow motion. Other ambulances and emergency personnel were now on the scene and helped others in the massive, smoldering wreckage. People were screaming and shouting from every direction for assistance. One car had burst into flames but the rain helped douse them. It was mass chaos as blood covered men and women flagged down emergency personnel. Lexx was oblivious to the chaos and screaming around her. She only heard the sound of her own heart pounding as she watched the EMT's working on her uncle. Monica finally stopped CPR as people shouted to her and Evan. She looked at Evan and shook her head.

"He's gone," Monica announced.

Lexx just stared at Brandon's motionless body as shock tore through her. She felt like she'd been stabbed through the heart. He wasn't dead. It wasn't possible! As if some bizarre survival instinct kicked in, Lexx bolted up from the pavement and ran for the limousine. Monica and Evan collected their bags and hurried to the next injured person as Lexx appeared from the limousine with her own black bag. Evan stopped before the crushed sports car molded against the garbage truck. He hurried to the front and looked through the broken windshield. Evan suddenly grimaced. What was left of the young man's head was unrecognizable, crushed into the glass of the windshield. He turned to Monica as she approached and shook his head in silent comment to her unasked question. His look caused her to grimace.

Lexx dove to Brandon's side with her black bag, dug through it, and tossed things haphazard from the bag. She found a pen and pulled it apart. As Monica turned, she saw Lexx feverishly ripping through more items in the bag. Lexx removed a bottle of alcohol and poured it over the pen and Brandon's neck. Monica appeared horrified and hurried back to her.

"What the hell are you doing?" Monica suddenly demanded while watching her.

Lexx barely heard the question and didn't have time for explanations. She ignored Monica and removed a scalpel from the bag. Monica gasped and lunged for Lexx and the scalpel in her hand. Both women struggled for the scalpel as the rain poured down upon them.

"His windpipe is obstructed!" Lexx cried out.

"His lung is collapsed!" Monica shouted back.

Lexx punched Monica in the mouth, sending her backwards and onto her backside. She didn't have time for this woman! Without hesitation, Lexx punctured Brandon's windpipe with the scalpel then skillfully inserted the tubing from the pen. Blood erupted from the tubing and around the hole in his windpipe but quickly subsided. Monica watched from where she sat on the pavement with a look of shock. Lexx punched Brandon in the chest with both fists and continued CPR. She covered his nose and mouth and blew into the pen despite the blood on it. Monica continued to stare and appeared almost frozen by her calculated actions and persistence. Lexx resumed chest compressions. A wheezing gurgled through the pen in his throat. Monica looked around for Evan and scrambled to her knees. She felt for a pulse and waved for Lexx to stop with the chest compressions.

"He's back," she announced then looked across the crash scene. "Evan," Monica cried out.

Lexx sank back on her feet and held her head in bloodied hands. Evan quickly returned with his bag. He seemed more shocked than Monica was to see the man now alive; or was it the blood-covered pen sticking from his neck that stunned him? Monica removed gauze in order to pack the crude trachea.

"Get the stretcher," Monica ordered to her partner. She then looked at Lexx, her eyes wide with amazement. "Who the hell are you?"

Lexx just trembled and appeared exhausted. Only a few minutes had passed. Lexx watched as the two EMT's lifted Brandon onto a stretcher, preparing to rush him away. Another motorist knelt alongside a barely dressed, severely injured young man lying face down several feet from the limousine. Evan and Monica rolled the stretcher toward him with Lexx following. Judging by his color, the young man's condition was in serious doubt.

"What do you have there?" Even asked the motorist.

"I'm afraid he's dead," the motorist replied.

"He's very much dead," Lexx casually informed them.

Evan, Monica, and the motorist looked at Lexx with bewilderment and possible shock to her callous comment regarding the dead man.

"We picked him up at the hospital morgue an hour ago," she announced.

Lexx indicated the writing on the back of the limousine. It read, 'Davenport Funeral Home'. Through the open back door, the stretcher could be seen strapped down, although half-cocked, inside the back of the limousine. The motorist suddenly jumped away from the corpse and stared at the dead man with horror. As Evan rushed the stretcher toward the awaiting ambulance, a pedestrian caught Monica by the arm.

"There are people trapped in that car," the female pedestrian cried out with alarm. "They're bleeding badly!"

Monica nodded Evan onward with the stretcher and followed the woman to the smashed Buick. Monica opened the driver's side door and immediately hesitated. Blood ran from Eric's neck in a waterfall down the front of his shirt. Monica applied pressure to the wound and felt his wrist with her free hand. She immediately frowned then looked back at the man's head. Upon closer inspection, it was clear his neck was broken. She removed her hand from his bleeding neck, allowing the blood to continue to pour from his jugular.

The female pedestrian appeared alarmed. "Aren't you going to do something for him?" she gasped.

"He's already dead," Monica informed her then hurried around the car to the passenger side. The pedestrian followed her. She attempted to open the door, but it wouldn't budge. Monica removed a tool that resembled a large screwdriver from her bag and rammed it into the door near the lock. With a couple of good thrusts, she was able to jolt the door open. Monica threw open the door and immediately checked Ava's pulse. She was still alive! She had several deep cuts and two broken arms that Monica was easily able to identify visually. She immediately applied gauze to the more severe cut on her head and looked around while holding the pad to the laceration.

"I need a stretcher over here!" Monica cried out.

Chapter Three

$\mathcal{E}$mmerich General Hospital was alive with activity and chaos in the dreary evening. News vans appeared to blanket the front of the building in what was possibly the worst accident in the history of their quiet town. Ambulances impatiently sounded their sirens at the news vans blocking their paths to the emergency room. Police cars were scattered throughout the area surrounding the hospital in an attempt to reign in busybodies lurking on every corner and control the media scattered about. The emergency waiting room was filled with anxious family members and those with less serious injuries seeking medical attention. It was going to be a long night for staff and patients. The nurses already appeared worn and frazzled, since most had been at the end of their twelve-hour shift when all hell broke loose. Those already working were forced to remain and help the evening shift.

Lexx paced the waiting room while clutching her wrapped wrist. She'd received her sprained wrist as a result from her CPR on Brandon and not from the crash itself. She knew it was only a sprain and had wrapped it herself with supplies from her own medical bag.

Apart from a slight concussion, she walked away nearly unscathed. Considering how many times the limousine rolled, her lack of injuries was a miracle. She didn't understand how her injuries could be so minor while her uncle seemed to be clinging to life and undergoing emergency surgery. She watched several stretchers being rushed through the waiting room and into the emergency room through the double doors. Several men and woman on the stretchers were covered in blood with injuries Lexx could only imagine were life-threatening. She knew there were other family members within the waiting room awaiting word on their loved ones the same as she was, but she couldn't even think about them. She was too worried for her own uncle. A man in his late twenties, Carson Davenport, entered the emergency room. He scanned the crowded room, saw Lexx, and hurried to her. She'd held it together fairly well until she saw her brother, Carson. As he pulled her into his arms, a flood of tears streaked her face and she sobbed uncontrollably.

"Lexx, are you okay?" Carson asked while clinging to her. He was obviously more worried about his little sister than he would ever lead on.

She reluctantly pulled away from her brother and attempted to wipe her tear-drenched face with trembling hands. "They took Uncle Brandon into surgery nearly two hours ago," she said while sniffing and tried to control her emotions. "I don't know if he'll be okay. He looked really bad."

"He's tough. He'll be okay," Carson assured her while keeping his hands on her shoulders. "Rolan is waiting downstairs with the hearse. Why don't you let him take you home?" His look was oddly tender and sympathetic compared with his usual brotherly attitude. "I'll stay here and wait for word on Uncle Brandon."

"No, I'll wait," she replied softly. "You'll need to help Rolan unload our friend back home. I won't be able to lift much anyway." She took a deep breath and grimaced slightly. She didn't want to ask the delicate question, but she had to know. "Did you get a look at our client? How bad was he?"

"We've restored worse," he replied with a tiny, reassuring smile. "I'll return as soon as we've put him on ice."

Carson gently kissed her on the forehead and looked into her eyes. "Uncle Brandon's going to be okay, I promise," he assured her.

Lexx nodded so Carson wouldn't worry about her, but she knew he was just saying those things to make her feel better. The ache in her heart and the lump in her throat had her convinced he wouldn't make it. She fought the tears waiting to be set free. She couldn't imagine life without her uncle. She'd never known a more levelheaded man. Strict and straight as they came, and yet he enjoyed corrupting his niece and nephew when they least expected it. Taking them to their first rated 'R' movie, giving them their first alcoholic drink, and buying her that trashy romance novel her mother wouldn't allow her to read. For Carson, it was cigars, beer, and girly magazines. After allowing Carson to overindulge, her brother successfully stayed away from tobacco and booze. A night puking his guts out cured him indefinitely. Unfortunately, there was no cure for Carson's insatiable appetite for female companionship. It was his one vice, and he intended to make the most of it.

✝

It was nearly midnight by the time Brandon was out of surgery and in the recovery room. Surviving the surgery was the first of many major hurdles for her uncle. Lexx sat in the chair alongside Brandon's bed while holding his hand and stared at the monitors and tubes. He remained unconscious the entire thirty minutes she'd been allowed to be by his side. He appeared slightly mangled but peaceful. The steady beat of his heartrate machine comforted her, reminding her that he was still alive. A man in his late forties wearing a scrub suit and lab coat, Dr. Gunther Sharp, entered the room with a clipboard in his hand. He saw Lexx by Brandon's bedside and offered a gentle smile.

"You must be the niece," he announced. "I'm Dr. Gunther Sharp, Chief Surgeon."

"Are you the one who operated on my uncle?"

"Yes," he replied. "Your uncle sustained several hairline fractures along his ribs, clavicle, and sternum. I suspect some of those injuries happened during CPR."

Lexx shifted with discomfort.

"It's common," he assured her. "He has some swelling in his brain from the contusion but no hemorrhaging. The next twenty-four hours are critical in these cases, but I'm optimistic about his recovery."

Her heart flip-flopped in her chest. It was the first optimistic statement she'd heard, and she couldn't deny it made her feel much better. "So you think he'll be okay?"

"Once he wakes, I believe he'll make a full recovery," Gunther announced with a hopeful smile. "He may be comatose for a couple of days, but with his head injury, that's not surprising." He saw her wrapped wrist and the bandage on her temple. "Have you been checked over?"

"Yeah, I'm fine," she replied and quickly brushed off any concern for her condition.

She couldn't tell him the truth. She didn't want to tell him that she had checked over herself. She didn't want him sending her for x-rays or tests. Lexx just wanted to remain by Brandon's bedside as long as they'd allow her to stay with him.

"Well, I'm going to prescribe home rest for you for the rest of the night," he announced sternly then offered a warm smile. "Go home. We'll look after your uncle."

"I think I should stay."

"We're moving him to ICU and you won't be allowed to visit for much longer anyway," he gently informed her. "Come back in the morning." His smile was charming but stern. "Doctor's orders. I insist."

Lexx eyed her uncle, considered the doctor's comment, and reluctantly nodded. It wasn't what she felt she should do, but she was physically exhausted and feeling extremely sore from the minor injuries she'd received from the accident as well. She uncertainly stood and headed for the door. She paused within the doorway to take one last look back at her uncle. She saw Dr. Sharp injecting something into Brandon's IV tube. It was curious, she thought. Most times, the nurses gave injections and medications. Of course, with how hectic the evening had been, she assumed they were shorthanded. As long as Brandon was recovering, she'd worry about minor details in the morning.

Chapter Four

The elegant, three-story Victorian home was in pristine condition and almost mansion-like with beautifully landscaped grounds. There were flowers, shrubs, and a small fountain to the front of the home set back on its large parcel of well-groomed land. Several gorgeous weeping willow trees lined the long driveway to a large, covered carport. The home would undoubtedly cause envy at first glance. Upon closer inspection, an elegant sign out front with the words, 'Davenport Funeral Home', dissuaded any envy. It was nearly two in the morning, yet several lights remained on within the mansion-like funeral home giving it an eerie glow. The large basement prep room resembled a sterile hospital morgue. An old-fashioned, gate-style elevator showcased the room just near the main door and stairs, giving it an old-world, country mansion charm. Lexx sat on a rolling pub stool and stared off at nothing in particular. Despite her exhaustion, she couldn't manage to sleep. She had too much on her mind. It had been a while since she had spoken and the silence was becoming uncomfortable. Lexx took a deep breath and finally spoke.

"I can't believe there were four fatalities and another dozen or more in critical condition," she announced softly and shook her head at the thought. "I'm really worried about my uncle, you know. He's been more of a father to me than my own father." She hesitated and shifted with discomfort. She didn't like how that sounded, even if it were true. "I mean, I love my father, don't get me wrong, but he was never really equipped to handle having a daughter." She drifted out a moment and finally looked up. "You know, I never told anyone that before, but I know you won't repeat it."

Lexx stared at the corpse of the young man lying on the metal prep table. It was the same young man, Roger, who had been ejected from the limousine during the accident. A sheet was pulled up to his neck, leaving only his head exposed. She sighed deeply and stood.

"Let's see what sort of damage we're looking at."

She pulled the sheet back, exposing his chest. He sustained postmortem and perimortem injuries to his chest, arms, and shoulders. A gaping wound had been crudely sutured on his chest. There were several scrapes and abrasions on his arms as well. Those injuries were from the car crash that originally claimed his young life. He had clung onto life for a few hours after the crash, surviving major surgery, but his injuries were too serious. He passed away yesterday morning. Lexx and Carson had heard about the crash on the news the previous night.

With the image they'd seen of the wreck, it was surprising he was in as good of shape as he was. The young man was no more than twenty-one years old. From a wealthy family, he was denied nothing, including the very expensive sports car he promptly wrecked three days after receiving the keys. His blood alcohol level was through the roof. A few bad decisions and his life was over before it really began. Lexx studied the dead man a moment longer. He was so close to her in age; it gave her chills. She needed to stop thinking about that. She picked up a scalpel and gently but with precision sliced into the jugular vein on his neck. There was minimal blood, and what blood there was, was thick and dark. She removed a large, metal device with a sharpened end. It resembled the most terrifying needle one could fathom.

She looked at the young man's face, sighed deeply, and then inserted the sharpened end into the incision in his jugular vein. It required some pressure to place it perfectly into the jugular but not so much as to shred through it. The other side entered the opposite end of the open jugular. She connected the plastic tubing to the huge needle sticking out of his neck and a second that ran down the side of the table. Lexx flipped a switch on the nearby machine. The machine hummed as embalming fluid was pushed through the plastic tube. She gently tapped the line. As the embalming fluid was forced in, the thick, dark coagulated blood was pushed out through the second tube, which emptied into a biohazard container beneath the table. She gently massaged his limbs to break up the rigor mortis, allowing the embalming fluid to push the old blood more easily through his body. As the machine hummed while gently doing its job, Lexx pulled back the sheet to expose the lower half of the young man's body. She groaned softly with distaste.

Postmortem scraps and torn flesh covered his legs and torso. His left leg had been broken and set from the accident that killed him, but his right foot sustained a compound fracture from the second accident. The broken anklebone protruded through the skin, leaving his foot severely twisted inward. Once again, there was very little blood with the postmortem injury. Lexx took a deep breath, grasped the leg and foot, and with a firm thrust, she reset the bone. The sound of grinding bone went straight through her. Normally, she received bodies from the hospital and they would take care of those sorts of injuries, but since this happened on her watch, it became her problem. She was slightly sickened. It was never the sight that bothered her, but the sound sent chills down her spine. She leaned on the table with both hands and inhaled deeply. Once the feeling of nausea passed, she straightened and concentrated on her job. She again looked at the young man's pale face.

"Don't worry about the scrapes from the accident," she informed him. "I'll have you as good as new for the funeral."

There was a soft tap on the door, startling her. Lexx looked across the basement prep room to a tall, lanky man in his late twenties. Rolan Falcon stood in the doorway not far from the elevator while watching her. His look was solemn but exhausted, and he looked as if he'd rolled out of bed.

"Do you have any idea what time it is? You should be getting some sleep," Rolan said gently.

"I can't sleep," she informed him. "If I don't keep busy, I'll go insane."

He folded his arms across his chest and casually leaned his shoulder against the doorframe. "Sounds like you're halfway there already."

"That was a private conversation between Roger and me."

Rolan straightened and studied her a moment. His look was sympathetic. "Want to talk about it?"

"What's there to talk about?" Lexx replied matter-of-fact without looking at Rolan. "We won't know anything until he comes out of the coma."

"Nothing to talk about?" Rolan gasped with surprise, allowing his arms to fall to his sides. "The man you idolized since you were in diapers died in front of you and you brought him back to life by cutting a hole in his windpipe." His look was stern. "You can't just keep that stuff inside."

"I'm pretty sure I can." Lexx returned to her work.

"Lexx--"

"Good night, Rolan," she chirped without looking at him.

Rolan frowned and left the room. She knew Rolan was well-meaning. He was a good man and a good friend. Carson and Rolan were roommates in college. Although they didn't exactly hit it off, a forced friendship was formed. When her brother introduced him to her, she and Rolan instantly connected. There was never anything romantic between them, but they shared a close friendship. Rolan was rarely ever serious, which balanced Lexx's excessively mature and serious personality. Basically, he forced her to act her age once in a while. When she needed an assistant to help with the 'behind the scenes' work, as Carson called it, she insisted they hire Rolan. His live-in status was a mixed blessing. She was thrilled; Carson was not. Lexx snapped out of her trance and again looked at the gaping wound left by the compound fracture on his ankle. She took a deep breath then reached for her medical sewing kit. If she wanted something to keep her busy and get her mind off her Uncle Brandon, her young client would do just that. He would require some major reconstruction. Thankfully, none of the damage was done to his face. She promised his mother an open casket, and she didn't want to disappoint the already grieving woman.

Chapter Five

$\mathcal{E}$mmerich General Hospital was oddly peaceful in the early morning hours. Considering the chaos just last evening, things were unusually quiet. Two ambulances were parked out front while awaiting emergency calls. The news vans were gone, for the moment, and there were few visitors in the early morning hours. The fourth floor ICU was almost peaceful with barely a soul around. Lexx stood before the UCI nurse's station and casually leaned on the tall counter while flipping through her uncle's chart. There weren't any nurses around or near the desk, and Lexx was tired of waiting for answers to her simple questions. She still wanted to know what that injection was her uncle received from Dr. Sharp, the man claiming to be Chief Surgeon. Doctor's didn't typically give shots, so it still bothered her that morning. With last evening's massive wreck, the nurses were undoubtedly swamped caring for critical patients and couldn't be bothered taking time out to answer her insignificant questions, at least that's how she felt.

At the opposite end of the hall, Monica talked with one of the orderlies, Alpert. They were the only other people Lexx noticed the entire time she stood outside the nurse's station. Despite her rugged appearance, Monica was a moderately attractive woman in her late twenties with dark nearly black hair. She seemed to be a tough woman with more than enough of her own mind not to accept anyone else's opinion. Perhaps Lexx was just soured on the woman after their altercation yesterday evening. The orderly she was talking with was lean, clean-cut, and built athletic. They made a nice couple, although they didn't interact on an intimate level, so their relationship was questionable. Lexx wondered if it was possible for any man to want the surly woman. Lexx decided it was best to mind her own business, particularly since what she was doing wasn't exactly authorized. Alpert finally ended the conversation and headed for one of the rooms in the opposite direction of the nurse's station. Monica saw Lexx with the chart in her hand, appeared irritated, and quickly approached the desk.

"What do you think you're doing?" Monica demanded with hostility.

Lexx had seen her approach and didn't bother looking up. The woman obviously didn't know the meaning of 'tactful' and preferred the 'get in your face' approach.

"Just a little light reading," Lexx casually replied.

Monica snatched the chart from her, barely startling Lexx. The anger clearly showed on Monica's face. "You can't just pick up charts and read them."

Despite her annoyance, Lexx showed restraint toward the insufferable woman. "That's my uncle's chart, and I have every right to know his condition."

"You want an update; you talk to the doctor or nurse," Monica snarled then indicated the chart while waving it. "This is confidential information."

"Not to me it isn't."

Lexx snatched the chart. Despite her surprise, Monica's reflexes prevented her from taking the chart. There was a minor struggle for control of the binder.

"I don't know who the hell you think you are--" Monica lashed out heatedly.

Lexx stared into her eyes with a venomous look. "I'm the one who kept my uncle from dying at the hands of an EMT who doesn't know a collapsed lung from a crushed windpipe!"

Monica appeared horrified by the comment then immediately turned enraged. "I'm calling security on your ass before I put my foot up it!"

Lexx grabbed Monica's wrist, twisted it, and removed the chart from her hand. Monica appeared stunned. She obviously hadn't expected the seemingly docile looking woman to come at her with such aggression.

"Don't push me," Lexx growled and walked away with the chart.

Monica suddenly tackled Lexx to the floor and both women screamed while wrestling each other for the chart. The sound attracted several people from nearby rooms. Voices were yelling over them. Lexx and Monica were roughly pulled apart and to their feet. Alpert held Lexx back, while a man with coal black hair in his early thirties and wearing a police uniform, Hill Burke, held Monica back. Lexx instantly calmed, but Monica thrashed against the handsome police officer.

"That's enough!" Hill shouted.

Monica stopped struggling, although she was cursing under her breath. Hill seemed to debate his next move then reluctantly released Monica. She spun to face him with hostility.

"She took a confidential chart," Monica lashed out. "I was trying to get it back when she assaulted me."

"Was that before or after you tackled her to the floor?" Hill casually asked.

Monica sneered at him. Lexx immediately realized there was a familiarity between the EMT and the officer. Depending upon their relationship, there was a good chance any argument would fall on deaf ears. Alpert released Lexx and picked up the discarded chart. Hill eyed the chart in Alpert's hand then glanced at Lexx while casually resting his hand on his gun belt.

"What's going on?" Hill demanded.

Lexx stood proudly and straightened her rumpled shirt from where the orderly held her. "My uncle is in critical condition, and I wanted to see what was being done for him," Lexx announced then indicated Monica with a sneer. "That crazy bitch is still a little pissy, because she nearly cost him his life yesterday."

Her words cut through Monica and nearly sent her into an uncontrollable rage. "I'm going to kick her ass if you don't get her out of here, Hill!"

First name basis wasn't going to play well in Lexx's favor. She was starting to wish she'd spent more time socializing and kissing ass like her brother. If she was lucky, Carson had some influential friends, because it was starting to sound like she'd be receiving a citation. The police officer was undeniably handsome, even Lexx with her limited dating experience had to admit as much. If he were dating the EMT, he'd undoubtedly side with her in a heartbeat. The law was the law, until it came down to the woman dating the law. Then the woman screwing the law had final say.

Hill glared at Monica and didn't appear pleased with her tone. He pointed a warning finger at her. "Secure that shit, Monica. I'm not in the mood," he launched back. "You're the only one who's out of control here."

Monica glared at Hill and appeared unusually hostile toward him. "Typical man; sticking up for the hot girl."

To Lexx's relief, they weren't lovers, which leveled the playing field. In fact, Monica didn't seem to like or respect the officer. The look on Hill's face was moderately enraged. The more Monica irritated the officer, the less likely he would side with her.

"As sheriff of Emmerich, I'm deeply offended by that comment," he growled lowly. "As your brother, speak to me like that again, and you won't live to see your next birthday."

Hill's words relieved Lexx. He was the EMT's brother. If their relationship was anything like hers and Carson's, Monica wasn't winning any arguments. Monica sneered and walked away while muttering a few hardcore curse words. Alpert handed Hill the chart and hurried after Monica. And there it was! The boyfriend was always the one chasing after the angry woman. Hill eyed the chart he held, tossed it onto the desk, and glared at Lexx. His cold gaze cut through her. What was it about police officers and principals? One look was enough to send a ripple of fear through her.

"Congratulations on rubbing my sister the wrong way," he boldly announced. "You've made an enemy for life."

She attempted to pretend his authority didn't intimidate her. It proved tough. He *was* intimidating. "Sorry, but your sister has a bad attitude."

"I'm aware of that, but you don't seem far behind," he informed her. "I'm sure you know patient files are confidential. You could have just walked away when she called you on it. That would have been the smart thing to do."

"I've had a very rough night. Thinking straight went out the window when the sun came up," Lexx remarked with little emotion. "The nurses aren't helpful, and I'm tired of waiting for the doctor."

He stared at her a moment but his expression didn't offer any insight to his thoughts. "Can you honestly tell me you understood anything you read?"

"I understood it all," she casually replied.

He appeared surprised while studying her. "Are you a doctor or something?"

"Not exactly," she replied. "I'm a mortician."

There was an awkward silence as he stared at her. It was the same look she received every time she told someone what she did for a living.

"A mortician?" he asked with some surprise.

She cleverly raised her brows and came back with her usual response to the familiar question coupled with *the look*. "Am I not creepy enough to be a mortician?"

Hill immediately fumbled from her bold comment and resumed his authoritative demeanor. "A mortician is a far cry from a doctor."

She grinned. "I'm smarter than I look."

They were approached by woman in her mid-thirties dressed in a lab coat. Dr. Tracy Kirby was a raven-haired beauty with olive skin and a flawless complexion. Her dark eyes and dark eyelashes stood out, further complemented by her ruby red lips. Lexx had to admit, she'd never seen a more beautiful woman. She was suddenly self-conscious about her own hair tossed carelessly into a ponytail with stray locks hanging in front of her eyes. If she thought the woman was beautiful, she wondered what the handsome sheriff was thinking at that moment. She couldn't even bring herself to cast a glance at him. Seeing men tripping over themselves around hot women was one of her pet peeves. Carson and Rolan were notorious for boyish giddy when confronted by hot women. Tracy paused before them and eyed both.

"I heard a commotion," she announced and appeared curious. "What's going on, Sheriff Burke?"

Hill picked up the chart and casually handed it to the attractive doctor. "I believe the young lady has some questions about her uncle's condition," he announced. Without a second glance, he walked away.

His lack of interest in the raving beauty surprised Lexx. Obviously, he was either gay or she was an ex-girlfriend. Disinterest didn't seem possible otherwise.

Tracy watched Hill walk away, looked at Lexx, and appeared bewildered. "Well, he's acting stranger than usual," she remarked then smiled with perfect, white teeth. "I'm Dr. Kirby. How can I help you?"

Lexx brushed off any thoughts of the relationship between the doctor and sheriff. "My uncle, Brandon Davenport, was in that car crash yesterday," she announced. "I wanted to know what medications he was being given, but the nurses were less than helpful."

"The ICU has been overwhelmed with patients since that accident," Tracy informed her. "The staff is stretched pretty thin."

She opened the chart and handed it to Lexx. "This is the list of medications your uncle is currently receiving. Routine stuff for someone in his condition. Heavy-duty painkillers, antibiotics, hydration fluids--" She offered a reassuring smile. "Let's go see him."

Lexx eyed the chart in her hands then followed the doctor to Brandon's room. She followed Tracy into the room and glanced at her uncle lying motionless in his bed. Brandon was still comatose with tubes and monitors surrounding him. Tracy picked up the clipboard, looked over it, and then checked the monitors while Lexx flipped through the chart with great interest. She skimmed through the less interesting parts and marveled at Dr. Sharp's horrible penmanship. She didn't find what she was looking for and glanced at the attractive doctor.

"What was that injection the surgeon gave him yesterday?" Lexx asked. "I don't see it listed."

Tracy looked at Lexx with mild confusion, took the chart from her, and browsed through it. She glanced at Lexx and shook her head.

"I assume it was some sort of painkiller, but it would have been an IV bag," she informed her. "We very rarely inject anything directly into the tubes, and I doubt Dr. Sharp injected it himself. That's the nurse's job."

"I know what I saw," Lexx informed her. "I thought it seemed strange, and it's been bugging me since last night."

Her comment seemed to strike the doctor as odd as well. She smiled and covered her confusion. "If it makes you feel better, I can check into it for you," Tracy announced.

"I'd appreciate that," Lexx replied then looked at her motionless uncle lying in his bed. "Is he improving?"

"Improving? Well, he's still in a coma," Tracy replied and set the chart aside. "With the head injury he received, he's going to be that way for quite some time. We're looking at possible brain damage--"

"Brain damage?" Lexx suddenly gasped and stared at the attractive woman with surprise. "Dr. Sharp believed he would make a full recovery in a couple of days." She felt her blood pressure spiking with her increased anxiety. "He didn't say anything about brain damage."

If Dr. Kirby was surprised by the comment, she covered it well. "Yesterday was a very chaotic and stressful day on all of us," Tracy gently informed her while noting Lexx's increased anxiety. "It's possible Dr. Sharp may have given you information on the wrong patient."

Lexx stared at her with horror as all expression drained from her face. "You don't expect my uncle to recover?"

Tracy stared at her and appeared equally surprised. She quickly composed herself and remained professional. "I'm very sorry you were misinformed about his condition, but there's always hope for recovery." She fumbled for something positive to add. "We'll know the extent once the swelling has gone down. A coma is the body's way of allowing itself to heal at its own pace. There's an excellent chance he'll come out of the coma," she announced then hesitated, "but there was damage."

Lexx stared at Tracy with her mouth hanging open and couldn't even speak. Carson entered the room with a smile and gave Lexx a hug, startling her.

"How is he?" Carson asked almost cheerfully, oblivious to the mood of the room.

Lexx held back her sobs, pulled from his arms, and shook her head. "I can't--" she gasped softly. "Talk to the doctor." Lexx ran from the room.

Chapter Six

 *T*he hospital basement corridor was drab and bland with cinder block walls painted white in an attempt to make it look more cheerful. The floor was basic concrete with a coat of paint to brighten the area. The basement was nearly silent with little to no activity. It wasn't a place most visited without good reason. Apart from those who worked downstairs, the traffic was relatively light, particularly early in the morning. Lexx sat on the floor not far from the morgue. She held her knees to her chest and sobbed softly into her knees. A shadow loomed over her.

"Lexx?" a male voice spoke over her.

Lexx sniffed, wiped the tears from her face, and looked up. A man in his early forties wearing a scrub uniform and a white lab coat stood over her. Lexx again sniffed and wiped her tears. Dr. Nathan Oswald crouched before her and appeared sympathetic.

"Is it Brandon?" he asked gently.

"The doctor just told me he has brain damage," she said softly and attempted to keep from crying.

"Oh, Lexx. I'm so sorry," he said sympathetically then raised his brows, "but don't you think you're getting ahead of yourself?

You've studied medicine." He placed his hand affectionately on her shoulder. "You know the brain is a funny little guy that can't be predicted. Brain damage could just mean he doesn't remember how to tie his shoes."

Lexx stared at Nathan and again wiped her eyes. His words seemed to help her relax. He was good at that. "Do you really think I'm overreacting?"

"Brandon is a tough son-of-a-bitch with an extremely thick head and a very high IQ," Nathan informed her. "To him, a little brain damage will just bring him closer to our level."

Lexx managed a soft laugh.

Nathan straightened and extended his hand to her. "Come on. I'll buy you a cup of tea."

Lexx accepted his hand and allowed him to help her to her feet. They approached the nearby door. The frosted glass window on the door had 'morgue' written on it. Beneath that, 'Dr. Nathan Oswald, Coroner'. Nathan opened the morgue door and allowed Lexx to enter ahead of him. A few minutes later, Lexx was sitting on the empty autopsy table while holding a cup of tea as she watched the coroner at the next table over. Nathan performed an autopsy on a man in his late fifties. Lexx watched him slice into the man's chest and crack open his sternum with a sternal saw, which looked like a glorified glue gun. He then placed the chest spreader into the opening, pried open his chest cavity, and exposed everything from the inside. As he skillfully probed and examined the dead man's internal organs, Lexx knew she was odd for finding his work so fascinating. The way he dove into a person's body with both hands left her mildly awestruck. Dr. Oswald was her hero.

"What happened to him?" she finally asked.

"Domestic dispute," he replied and cast a glance at her. "He lost."

"That's awful."

"Eh, not really," Nathan replied callously with a shrug. "Judging by the condition of his wife, I'd say he had it coming. Any man raising his hand to a woman in that manner is living on borrowed time, if you want my opinion." He sighed deeply and continued with his work. "Sheriff Burke wants me to cross my 'T's' and dot my 'I's' on this one. Our dead guy's bastard of a brother is pushing for the wife's arrest, but the sheriff has been to that house enough to know she was defending herself."

"How did she do him in?"

Nathan motioned Lexx over. Lexx jumped off the autopsy table with a little too much enthusiasm and approached the dead man with his chest spread apart. Nathan stepped back and studied her while she visually examined the body. Although she couldn't see it, he watched her with an odd fascination. Lexx finally pointed to a small hole in the opened chest.

"I'm guessing that hole did him in," she responded then eyed him. "What caused it?"

"You tell me," he replied.

Nathan handed Lexx a spectrum and challenged her with a sly smirk. She grinned her acceptance to the challenge, took the spectrum, and gently poked around beneath the tissue.

"Strange little hole," she announced and appeared bewildered while studying the puncture. She looked back at Nathan while raising her brows with surprise. "Knitting needles?"

Nathan chuckled softly and appeared pleased. "You missed your calling, sweetheart."

There was a knock on the door as it opened, causing both to look up. Hill entered, saw the open body on the table, and immediately turned away.

"Oh, God--"

Nathan was amused by Hill's reaction to the corpse and grinned teasingly at Lexx. "The sheriff is a tad squeamish."

"Then let's hope he never has to shoot anyone," Lexx announced.

"Hey, I can handle blood," Hill stated firmly, offended by the remark. He finally looked at them while attempting to keep from looking at the dead man on the table. "When a man's insides are on the outside, that's where I draw the line."

"Then you aren't going to want to see this--" Nathan announced while removing the stomach from the body.

Hill eyed the organ within the coroner's bloodied, gloved hands and quickly left the room. Nathan chuckled and set the stomach on the counter.

Lexx gave him a disapproving frown. "That was cruel."

Nathan casually leaned on the counter over the stomach and eyed Lexx. "Sheriff Burke needs to get that ugly stick out of his ass. He has no respect for people like us."

"People like us?"

"Those who make their living sitting up with the dead," he remarked curtly. "We're the creepy basement dwellers carving up bodies then sewing them back together."

She stared at him a long moment then groaned softly. "God, I wish I could deny what you just said, but I work in the basement too. Even Carson gives me funny looks from time to time."

The coroner suddenly seemed curious. "Wasn't he your father's golden child?"

"It was my father's hope that Carson would take over the family business, but Carson is almost as squeamish as Sheriff Burke, I'm afraid," she announced with a sigh. "I know what you mean though. I get those looks all the time. *'You're a mortician? You don't look like a mortician.'* What the hell is that supposed to mean?" she suddenly demanded. "What is a mortician supposed to look like? Igor?"

"Back when I was in high school, many, many years ago, I played football and dated cheerleaders," he announced with reflective glee then frowned. "Now women lose interest the moment I tell them what I do for a living."

"Ironic, Brandon and I were having the same discussion just before the accident," she replied with some sadness at the mention of Brandon. "He told me I needed to date more." She frowned and folded her arms across her chest. "I couldn't bring myself to tell him the real reason why I don't date."

"The look?"

"Exactly."

"*You're a what?*" Nathan mocked in a high-pitched squeal.

She laughed softly. "You've mastered it."

"We should go out sometime," he teased while grinning. "Imagine the talk."

Lexx laughed softly at the comment then saw the uncomfortable way he shifted. She turned serious and studied him. "Wait--are you asking me out?"

He seemed tense then casually shrugged. "That depends. Would you say yes?"

"Huh, well, I never actually gave it much thought," she replied then considered it. "I mean, I certainly wouldn't go out on a date with Brandon lying in a hospital bed."

"No, of course not," he agreed and again shifted. "How about after he's on his way to recovery? Maybe we could have dinner some time."

There was an awkward silence. Lexx finally smiled and nodded. "Yes, we could do that."

"Then it's a date--on some later date," he teased.

Lexx smiled and laughed softly with him. There was obviously a huge age gap between them, but she didn't see the harm in going out with Nathan. She admired him, and they were compatible. Carson would obviously never approve because of the age difference, but a date didn't mean they were getting married. Sadly, Lexx didn't even remember the last time she'd been on a date. The prospect of having sex again before she died sounded appealing. As she watched Nathan carve open the stomach like a Thanksgiving turkey, she was reminded that admiration didn't equal sexual attraction. There was nothing physically wrong with Nathan, and he certainly wasn't unattractive. Despite spending long hours locked in his basement retreat, Nathan still retained some of his muscle tone from his high school football days.

Physically, he was pleasing to the eyes, and she had to admit his skill with a scalpel was an amazing sight to behold. She just didn't feel an overwhelming desire to rip his clothes off and have her way with him. She was aware of his attraction toward her, but she also knew that men could sexually desire just about any woman if they really put their mind to it. Nathan was in dire need of a sexual relationship. Rolan would retell dirty jokes and sexual innuendoes Nathan shared with him when he'd stop by to pick up a deceased client. Still, it had been a long time since she'd felt sexual desire for any man. She wasn't even sure she believed in love anymore. Love, to her, was just something that came with time. It was entirely possible she could learn to love Nathan in that way.

Chapter Seven

*T*racy stood by the nurse's station on the fourth floor ICU and wrote a doctor's order in one of the charts. She glanced across the unit and saw Dr. Gunther Sharp enter one of the patient's rooms, which was highly unusual. Tracy appeared curious, set her chart aside, and headed across the floor to the room Dr. Sharp entered. She stopped just short of the door, hesitated with added suspicion, and glanced through the window into the room. She witnessed Dr. Sharp injecting something into the IV tube of one of the female crash patients. He capped the syringe, placed it in his lab coat pocket, and then turned for the door. Protocol for needles required they be disposed in the red biohazard sharps containers attached to the walls in each room. Recapping a syringe let alone placing it in one's pocket was a gross violation of safety. It seemed unfathomable that he'd knowingly break protocol. Tracy quickly darted away from the window, pretended to approach from the opposite direction, and nearly collided with him. He jumped from their near miss and chuckled softly.

"They really should put up stoplights," he teased. Despite his jovial mood, he seemed oddly tense having been caught coming from that particular room.

"Making rounds, Dr. Sharp?" she asked in an attempt to sound cheerful but failed.

"Just checking on some of the crash victims I operated on yesterday," he replied then indicated the critical woman in the room. "What's the story on that one?"

"Ava Martin?" Tracy questioned. "I'm afraid she's not doing well. She's still in a coma, and it appears that her brain damage is severe." She offered a defeated sigh and folded her arms across her chest. "If she wakes, she's going to be non-functioning. It's a shame, really."

"Tragic. Her surgery went so well too," Dr. Sharp remarked. "Keep me posted on the condition of those from the car wreck, Dr. Kirby."

"Certainly, Dr. Sharp."

Gunther walked past her and down the corridor toward the elevator. Tracy skeptically watched him leave then entered the patient's room. She removed the patient's clipboard from the wall and flipped through it. She shook her head with disbelief and flipped through it again. There was no documentation of the injection he gave her or even that he had visited. Tracy replaced the clipboard with disgust, approached the IV bag on the pole, and studied the contents. She looked at Ava Martin lying unconscious within her hospital bed. She had lacerations along her face and a large shaved patch on her head, which revealed the large sutured wound. The woman in her early thirties spent hours in surgery having fragments of metal removed from her head. The operation had been a success but the damage was severe. At that point, there was nothing anyone or any injection could do to save the woman. Recovery was waking from the coma in a non-functioning capacity. The brain damage was severe. What did Dr. Sharp expect an injection would do for the poor woman?

Tracy released the IV bag and sank deep into thought. As she walked out of Ava's room, she noticed an orderly in his late thirties, Newman, watching her. She made eye contact with him and didn't look away. Newman immediately turned and headed down the hall. Tracy stared after him while placing her hands in her lab coat pockets. He'd obviously caught her attention.

†

*O*t was two days later. The large, elegant viewing room at the Davenport Funeral Home was filled with flowers. White wooden folding chairs were neatly arranged before the open casket toward the far end. The young man from the prep room was dressed in an expensive suit looking peaceful within the top-of-the-line casket. Lexx arranged a boutonniere on his lapel while Rolan finished setting up the chairs. The young man looked natural and nearly lifelike. Applying make-up to the deceased was an art form, particularly when applied to men. With men, it had to look natural. Lexx would have loved taking credit for Roger's flawless make-up, but Rolan was the true artist. He had a talent with the men in particular. With the women, not so much. He tended to go overboard, particularly with the lipstick. He had a fondness for bright red, shiny lips. Lexx wasn't sure where his obsession came from, but every year at Christmas, he'd buy her a tube of bright red lipstick. She had eight brand new tubes in her dresser drawer. He had to know she rarely wore make-up and certainly never bright red lipstick, but, apparently, he kept hoping she would one day.

"It's going to be one hell of a turnout tomorrow," Rolan announced while raising his brow in suggestion. "I hear our boy was very popular at his college."

"I hope Carson remembered to contact the police for the traffic stops," she remarked and released a defeated sigh. "The streets are going to be a disaster." There was an odd silence between them as they worked. She suddenly turned and looked at Rolan. "I can't believe Carson went out on a date tonight. If it isn't disrespectful enough with Uncle Brandon lying unconscious in the hospital, it's terrible for him to leave us here with all this prep work for a funeral of this size."

"Well, that's Carson," Rolan replied. "Brandon would be laying odds on whether or not Carson comes home tonight."

Lexx glanced at the clock and raised her brows. "Well, it is about that time."

"Yep, he's either bagging his babe or coming home with a pouty face," Rolan teased and held back his laugh. Betting on Carson's scoring record was an excellent way to pass time. "I guess we should be happy he doesn't bring them home. Nothing makes me feel like less of a man then listening to Carson screw some chick's brains out."

"His dates tend to be turned off the moment they see the word 'funeral home' outside," she replied.

The front door was heard opening. Lexx and Rolan exchanged looks and snickered softly.

"Oh, he struck out," Rolan teased. "We have a long evening of his pouty face to look forward to."

Carson appeared in the viewing room doorway, sensed their gossiping and glared at both with disapproval. "Were you talking about me again?"

Lexx turned and was about to joke with him when Tracy appeared alongside him. Lexx's expression dropped as she stared with surprise. "Dr. Kirby?"

Rolan suddenly looked up and stared with disbelief. The young doctor looked even more radiant dressed up for her date. Lexx suddenly felt like a rag doll dressed in her finest t-shirt and worn jeans. Perhaps if she hadn't been wearing her pink, fuzzy slippers she could have retained some of her dignity. How was it possible for a woman to be that attractive?

"You remember my sister, Lexx," Carson announced then indicated Rolan. "And this is her assistant, Rolan."

"Yes, I've seen you around the hospital," Tracy said politely to Rolan.

He appeared unable to speak and instead stared at the gorgeous woman with his mouth hanging open, possibly hung up on her ruby red lips. Tracy noticed the young man in the casket, and her expression dropped to that of surprise.

"Oh, I remember him," Tracy announced. "I operated on him after his car accident."

"Blood alcohol through the roof," Rolan informed her.

"Rolan--" Lexx scolded softly.

"It's okay. I sort of suspected that myself," Tracy replied then approached the casket. She looked over the young man then back at Lexx. "He looks good."

"Most of his injuries were from the neck down," Lexx informed her.

"Lexx is very talented," Carson announced proudly. "She can restore bodies in almost any condition."

"It's not a talent worth bragging about," Lexx muttered.

Carson placed his arm around Tracy and forced a smile. "Before this conversation turns gross, Tracy and I are going to have drinks in the lounge."

Tracy offered a smile and waved as Carson guided her away. Rolan watched her backside as she left the room, while Lexx wondered how the woman could walk in those stiletto heal shoes.

She hoped she wasn't expected to wear high heels on her date with Nathan. Lexx and Rolan exchanged looks.

"Dr. Kirby?" Lexx nearly gasped while raising a brow. "Seriously?"

Rolan sneered and appeared irritated. "He brought her home just to rub it in," he scoffed. "I can't believe she'd go out with him."

"Had you asked her out?" Lexx knew if he hadn't, he most certainly had thought about it. Seeing those big, ruby red lips must have sent Rolan into spasms of sexual desire.

"No, but I've seen her in passing on the way to the morgue," Rolan informed her. "Every man who breathes has asked out Dr. Kirby at one time or another." He raised his brows knowingly. "Her track record is very selective."

"Huh?"

Lexx looked toward the empty doorway. Her thoughts momentarily strayed to Sheriff Burke's non-reaction to the gorgeous, young doctor. She was almost certain he would fit into her selective list. Carson on the other hand--?

"You're right," she remarked. "How did he get her to go out with him let alone come back here?"

She almost felt bad for saying that aloud. Carson was attractive in his own rights, but he certainly wasn't in the same league as Sheriff Burke. Although, her brother could be quite charming when he wanted to be.

"Life is filled with bitter irony," Rolan said with a dreary sigh while keeping his eyes on the empty doorway.

Those lips would undoubtedly be on his mind the remainder of the night. Of course, they would. Even Lexx was having a difficult time fighting off the image of the ravishing doctor. She hated to admit she was jealous, but what woman wouldn't be?

Chapter Eight

It was two days later. The fourth floor ICU remained fairly quiet and without drama since the evening of the massive car wreck. Tracy approached the nurse's station with a fast, determined walk while clutching a clipboard with a death grip. She approached a young nurse, Rose, who wrote in a chart behind the desk. Rose hadn't even seen her approach and appeared startled as the clipboard struck the desktop.

"Rose, am I seeing this right?" Tracy suddenly announced, causing the nurse to jump at her tone. "Four of the patients from the car wreck died last night?"

Rose sympathetically nodded. "They took a turn for the worse shortly after midnight."

"Nearly all our critical patients from the car wreck have died in the last four days," Tracy remarked and defiantly shook her head. "That's a bit coincidental, don't you think?" She didn't wait for the nurse to respond and began scribbling on the physician's order page in the chart. "I want full tox screens done on all of them. If there was a medication screw-up, I want to know about it."

"All of them?" Rose asked with surprise.

"Yes, you heard me," she snapped and grabbed another chart to write the blood work order. "Contact the coroner immediately and have him hold all the bodies." She cast the clipboard onto the nurse's station desk with disgust. "How many patients from the car wreck are still in ICU?"

"Just the two," Rose replied. "Brandon Davenport and Ava Martin."

"I want their medications reviewed and complete blood work done on both of them as well," she instructed firmly. "I want to know every drug found in their systems."

Rose appeared slightly concerned and quickly nodded while springing into action. "Yes, Dr. Kirby."

It wasn't like the doctor to react with such vigor, and the nurse reacted accordingly. Tracy stormed away from the desk as Rose snatched the phone to call Nathan. Rose watched her leave and appeared bewildered.

†

*G*unther walked out of his corner office on the fifth floor. The fifth floor was mostly home to doctor's offices and outpatient specialists. The chief surgeon headed down the corridor for the elevators. He waited only a moment for the elevator to arrive, pressed the fourth floor button, and disappeared behind the closing doors. Tracy looked around the corner as the doors closed, saw that Gunther was gone, and then hurried for his office. She tried to open the door, but it was locked. As if anticipating it, she removed a skeleton key, unlocked the old door, and quickly slipped inside. Tracy hurried for the large, antique desk, flopped into the leather chair, and searched every drawer quickly and quietly. She saw an old set of keys and appeared curious. She picked up the keys and looked around. Her eyes fell upon the old secretary off to the side of the office. She approached the antique cupboard and inserted one of the keys in the lock. It unlocked the top. She opened it and appeared disappointed.

There were decanters, a few bottles of alcohol, and several mixers within the cupboard. Why lock up his alcohol? No one had keys to his office. She tried different keys and finally found one that unlocked the first drawer. The only item within the drawer was a large, metal case. She needed a separate key to unlock the case.

Something seemed wrong. What was within the case that it had to be locked so securely? She found the key to unlock the case and opened it. It contained a notebook and several viles secured in padded slots. Each vile had its own label with Dr. Sharp's distinctive scribbled handwriting. She removed the notebook and flipped through it. Names of the patients and which injection they received were listed in detail. The word 'deceased' was written behind each of them. At the bottom of the page were the names Brandon Davenport and Ava Martin. Their names were the only two without deceased written behind them.

As Tracy scanned the list of names, she saw the names of the four crash victims who'd died last night. He'd given them all injections of some sort. What he was up to almost didn't even matter. He was experimenting on critical patients, which was gross negligence no matter what his excuse. Tracy removed one of the viles and placed it in her lab coat pocket. She kept the notebook and shut the drawer. She quickly returned the keys to the desk drawer where she'd found them and slipped out of the office. As she turned, she nearly collided with the same orderly she'd seen on the fourth floor outside Ava's room. Tracy appeared slightly startled to see the orderly but forced a false smile.

"You startled me, Newman," she announced and collected herself. "Have you seen Dr. Sharp? He's not in his office."

"He's making rounds in ICU," Newman said then indicated the notebook she held against her chest. "Did you take that from his office?"

Tracy forced the notebook into her pocket and took an authoritative tone. "If you see Dr. Sharp, tell him I'm looking for him."

As she walked past him, Newman grabbed her arm.

She glared at him and became hostile. "Unhand me or I'll call security."

Newman released her arm without hesitation. Tracy walked halfway down the corridor then uncertainly looked back. Newman followed her. She walked faster toward the elevator. The orderly picked up his pace. She removed her cell phone and pressed a button. When she looked back, Newman ran for her. Tracy cried out and ran for the elevator. She frantically pressed the button. The orderly grabbed her and pulled her into the nearby stairwell as she fought him. Newman slammed Tracy against the wall and clutched her throat to keep her from screaming. He removed the notebook and shook his head.

"You shouldn't take things that don't belong to you," he remarked in a low tone.

Tracy stared into his eyes while gasping for her breath as she clutched his hand on her throat. She scratched his hand while attempting to pull free from his grip. Newman suddenly tossed her down the stairs. Tracy's scream was deafened by the sound of her body thumping against the metal steps. She struck the landing halfway down and lay motionless. Newman turned and was about to leave the stairwell when he heard her moan faintly. He groaned softly, hurried down the stairs, and tossed her onto her back. He checked for a pulse. She was unresponsive but still alive. Newman grabbed her head and prepared to snap her neck when he heard shouting from the stairwell below.

"It sounded like someone fell! Hurry!" Rose was heard shouting from two floors down.

Newman straightened with alarm and stared over the railing to the stairs below. There was a wet spot on his pants leg where he knelt alongside the doctor. There was a matching spot on Tracy's lab coat pocket. He subconsciously brushed the spot on his pants and then wiped the sweat from his face. He hurried up the steps as someone also ran up them from ground level. Newman bolted through the stairwell door and quietly closed it behind him. He hurried along the fifth floor corridor while clearing his throat then coughed several times.

Rose and the EMT, Evan, hurried up the stairs and saw Tracy lying on her back on the landing.

"Dr. Kirby," Rose gasped with horror.

Evan briefly checked her vitals and looked at Rose. "She's breathing," he announced with concern in his voice. "We're going to need a stretcher and a trauma board."

Rose nodded and ran back down the stairs. Evan remained on his knees alongside the young doctor and visually accessed her injuries. Moving a fall victim could do more damage, possibly causing paralysis. He cleared his throat several times then coughed. The spot on Tracy's lab coat was almost completely dry already, so Evan didn't even notice it.

The fourth floor stairway door flew open as Rose ran into the corridor from the stairwell and grabbed a nearby stretcher. She coughed several times then cleared her throat, almost stopping her in her tracks.

"I need help! Stat!" Rose shouted and again cleared her throat. She began pushing the stretcher toward the stairwell.

Alpert was the first to approach and ran to catch up to her. "What's happening?"

"Dr. Kirby fell down the stairs," she cried out. "We need a trauma board!"

Alpert turned and ran in the opposite direction for the nearest trauma board. He ran back to Rose, tossed the board on top of the stretcher, and helped her maneuver it through the stairway door.

Chapter Nine

Alpert, Rose, and Evan rushed Tracy on a stretcher through the emergency room corridor. It had only taken the trained professionals a few minutes to put her in traction and transport her onto the stretcher. They wasted little time rushing her to the emergency room. Gunther had been alerted to the situation and hurried toward them, meeting them halfway. He checked the unconscious doctor's pupils with a penlight as he ran alongside the stretcher to emergency room four. They carefully and efficiently striped her of her clothing and dressed her in a hospital gown, keeping her neck in traction until they could scan her for fractures. Rose assisted Gunther while Alpert placed the doctor's clothing into a bin. He carefully folded her lab coat to fit it inside the bin. He suddenly cried out with surprise and instinctively pulled his hand back. Blood seeped through the tiny cut in his latex glove. Alpert carefully opened the lab coat pocket and dumped the broken vile into a dish. Rose approached and saw the blood as he vigorously scrubbed his hands with betadine solution.

"Are you bleeding?" Rose suddenly asked with alarm while attempting to look at his bleeding finger.

Dr. Sharp appeared alarmed and looked at them across the room from the exam table. "What happened?" Gunther suddenly demanded.

Alpert shook his head and waved them off with little emotion. "Just a broken vile," he announced. "It didn't contain blood. Just an empty vile. It's nothing."

"Empty or not, you'd better bag that just in case," Rose scolded her friend.

"Yeah, I've got it," Alpert muttered.

Rose cleared her throat several times then coughed. She shook her head and again cleared her throat.

Alpert eyed her while drying his freshly scrubbed hands. "You getting sick?"

"Just a scratchy throat," she replied and gently massaged her throat. "This place is so dry."

"Let's get her to x-ray," Gunther ordered and began waving them from the room.

Rose and Alpert wheeled Tracy from the room on the stretcher. Gunther glanced at the counter and uncertainly stared at the broken vile in the sealed, biohazard bag. A bewildered look crossed his face. He cast a glance toward the door, watching as Rose and Alpert disappeared with the stretcher. Once they were out of sight, he took the biohazard bag.

†

It was late afternoon. The fourth floor ICU seemed fairly quiet with limited activity. It may have had something to do with four less patients requiring critical care after the recent deaths. Lexx stepped off the elevator and headed toward Brandon's room. A loud commotion suddenly erupted, startling her. Nurses and orderlies began scrambling from every corner of the floor followed by a page over the intercom.

"Dr. Sharp to ICU, stat," came the frantic nurse's voice.

Lexx watched the corridor now alive with activity and felt her heart suddenly pounding in her chest as she watched them run toward her uncle's room.

"Please, no," Lexx whispered softly and was suddenly unable to move.

The swarm of orderlies and nurses ran into the room just before her uncle's room. Lexx felt relief even if it was at the expense of some other poor soul. She continued past the room filled with emergency staff, peered in as she passed, and then headed for Brandon's room. Within Ava Martin's room, Rose and another nurse cleared the rolling table and any unnecessary equipment out of the way. Newman pushed the crash cart closer to the bed. Ava's heart had stopped, which was indicated by the relentless humming coming from the heart monitor. Rose inserted a tracheal tube down her throat, attached the portable resuscitation bag, and squeezed the bag, filling her lungs with oxygen. Dr. Sharp ran into the room as the second nurse prepared the defibrillator paddles. He took the paddles from the nurse.

"Clear!"

Everyone stepped back from Ava. He zapped her with the paddles, causing her body to jolt in the bed. Her heart monitor began beeping, causing everyone to sigh with relief. Dr. Sharp returned the paddles to the nearby machine and pat Rose on the shoulder.

✝

Lexx sat alongside Brandon's bed and held his hand while he remained comatose. The commotion from Ava's room next door had ceased, so she assumed the woman had survived yet another trauma. Lexx watched her uncle in silence and wondered if he would soon share the same fate as the others. Seeing him unresponsive was frightening to her. She knew he was alive, yet it was almost as if he wasn't. Lexx feared seeing him on her prep table, cold and lifeless. It was a thought she couldn't fathom.

"I don't know if you can hear me, but I need you to come back to me," she said softly with a quiver in her voice. "Rolan's trying to fill your shoes, and he's making me absolutely insane. I think he misses you almost more than I do."

There was no response and nothing to indicate her words made it through to whatever world he was stranded. A tiny smile crossed her face despite the tear rolling down her cheek.

"Hey, I have a date," she announced in a failed attempt to sound cheerful. "I thought you might be happy to hear. Of course, I'll have to postpone it until you're back with us." She shrugged and attempted a soft laugh. "So if you want me to go on that date, you'll need to wake up."

There was still no response from the motionless man. She didn't think it would actually work, but she was willing to try almost anything to bring him back.

"You have a really hot doctor," Lexx announced. "You'll definitely want to check her out. Although, Carson's currently your competition."

Carson slowly entered the room while rubbing his eyes and attempting to keep from losing control. Lexx saw his red, puffy eyes, noted his distressed mood, and felt alarm rushing through her. Something had obviously happened, but she didn't know what it could be. It wasn't Brandon, since she was sitting alongside him the last half hour.

"What's wrong?" Lexx suddenly asked as she slowly stood to face him.

"The nurse just told me," Carson said softly as his voice cracked and finally made eye contact. "Tracy fell down the stairs. She's in critical condition."

Lexx stared at him with surprise as horror filled her eyes. "Oh, my God," she gasped. "I can't believe that. Did they say how it happened?"

He shook his head and sniffed. "Dr. Sharp thinks the next twenty-four hours will give us a better idea of her condition," he informed her while fidgeting and ran his trembling fingers through his hair. "She, uh, has a dozen or more broken bones." He stared into his sister's eyes. "Do you think you can sneak a peek at her chart? They, uh, won't really tell me anything. Four dates doesn't qualify as a significant other."

"They aren't going to let me near her chart, Carson," Lexx gently informed him. She wished she could say something more to console him, but she knew there was nothing she could do. "Not a doctor; not one of their own."

Carson attempted to hold back his sobs. "You know, this is just so typical. We clicked," he interjected while haphazardly wiping the tears from his eyes. He was in a state between sorrow and rage. "I felt so comfortable with her, and now this--"

She felt the pain her brother was going through, but the words that came out of her mouth were the same lies she was being told about Brandon.

"You need to have a little faith, Carson," she said gently. Her own words almost caused her to grimace. She had little to no faith at that moment herself.

"When your business is death, it's hard to have faith in life," he replied callously.

He didn't have to tell her. She already knew that. She had no words to comfort him. Lexx placed her arms around her brother and held him. He clung to her and sobbed softly. It was possibly the first time she'd ever known him to cry. He obviously had deeper feelings for the woman he'd just started dating than he'd confided to her.

Chapter Ten

$\mathcal{M}$onica, Evan, and Alpert sat on one of the benches outside the emergency room near where the ambulances were parked. It was another quiet morning, and they preferred it that way. Monica drank take-out coffee from a paper cup while Evan and Alpert smoked their cigarettes and discussed the hot topic from last night. Dr. Kirby's tumble down the stairs was all anyone was talking about that morning.

"Sounds like more damage than I expected," Evan reported. "Usually when someone falls down steps, they try to brace their fall. To me, it looked like she dived down them."

"Dr. Sharp didn't make that assumption," Alpert remarked with surprise. "Are you sure you saw right?"

"We've seen a lot of falls in our job," Evan informed him. "You start recognizing which ones are accidents and the ones where someone had a little help."

Alpert appeared stunned and stared at his friend. "You suspect someone pushed her down the stairs?"

"That's insane," Monica finally chimed in. "Who'd toss a doctor down the stairs?"

Evan was about to respond then suddenly cleared his throat several times and coughed. He removed a throat lozenge and sucked on it. Alpert puffed on his cigarette then coughed several times as well. Monica glared at both men with annoyance then moved further down the bench from them.

"If either of you gets me sick, I'll kick your ass," Monica snapped.

Alpert glared at Evan and cleverly raised his brow. "Your girlfriend is bitchier than usual this morning. You're slacking in your nightly duties."

Monica cast a glare at Alpert. She wasn't humored.

"She's not my girlfriend," Evan bluntly announced then grinned with amusement. "I wouldn't date a woman with balls bigger than mine."

Both men laughed at Monica's expense. Monica glared her disapproval at the comment. It was a chilling look that almost stopped their laughing. Almost.

"If you girls are finished doing your nails, can we get back to work?" Monica snarled.

†

*T*he Davenport Funeral Home was quiet it the early morning. The country setting with few homes nearby was the ideal location for the nature of their business. The entire area was usually serene and with limited activity. Lexx wearily shuffled into the kitchen. She'd had another sleepless night. Since Brandon had been in the coma, she barely slept more than a few hours each night. She saw Carson slumped over the island counter while holding his head. He looked like he hadn't slept at all. Lexx knew he'd been through a lot the last few days between Uncle Brandon and Dr. Kirby. She tensed slightly as she stared at him. He seemed particularly sedate, telling her something had happened.

"Is everything okay?" Lexx gently asked.

"The hospital called--"

Lexx stared at him in silence. Her heart nearly pounded out of her chest. She feared the words that were certain to follow. Something happened to their uncle!

"Tracy died," he said softly.

The news was heartbreaking, and she felt terrible for her brother. She couldn't deny some small relief that the bad news hadn't involved Brandon. She shamed herself for even thinking such things. Lexx placed her arms around Carson's neck from behind and held him.

"Oh, Carson. I'm so sorry," she whispered.

The cordless phone lying on the counter near Carson rang. Both looked at the phone as if it would bite them.

"Let the machine get it," Lexx finally said and attempted to console her brother.

He wiggled free from her hug and showed little emotion. "No, you should answer it."

She picked up the phone, pressed the button, and placed it to her ear. "Davenport Funeral Home, Lexx speaking," she announced in the most pleasant voice she could manage. There was a tense moment of silence. She immediately fidgeted. "Mr. Kirby, I'd just heard. I'm so sorry for your loss." Carson eyed Lexx. They exchanged looks of surprise. "Uh, Carson just walked in. May I put you on hold?" She awaited his approval. "Thank you." Lexx pressed a button, looked at Carson, and appeared tense. "Tracy's family wants us to handle her final arrangements," she informed him. "If you don't want--"

"No, that's fine, Lexx. I'm okay, really," he replied then exhaled deeply. "Make the arrangements and go with Rolan to the morgue."

It was obvious he wasn't okay with taking the case. Carson stood and left the kitchen without another word. Lexx watched him leave and couldn't help but frown. Handling Tracey's final arrangements was going to be difficult for her and mortifying for Carson. She didn't know why he agreed to it. It wasn't as if they needed the work, and Tracy's father would have understood once he heard she'd been seeing Carson. She frowned and stared at the cordless phone with the 'hold' light blinking at her. She inhaled deeply and picked up the phone.

"Hello, Mr. Kirby--?"

†

*N*athan sat at the counter near the back of the morgue with his morning coffee. He looked refreshed and well rested. It was another beautiful day in the hospital morgue with just a hint of formaldehyde in the air. The knock on the door disrupted his perfect, quiet morning. He looked up as the door opened to reveal

Alpert and Newman.   The orderlies pushed a sheet-covered stretcher into the morgue.   Nathan uncertainly stood, stared at the stretcher, and appeared almost sedate.

"Is that--?"

"Yeah, it's Dr. Kirby," Alpert said in a dreary tone.   The staff had all taken her death hard.   "The funeral home will be along later today to pick her up."

Nathan attempted to hide his frown.   He approached the freezers, opened one of the doors mid-row, and pulled out the metal slab.   Newman and Alpert removed the sheet to reveal Tracy's pale, lifeless body in a hospital gown.   Her exposed legs revealed a large black and blue mark that was undoubtedly a broken bone.   Stitches were visible on her lower, left arm where Dr. Sharp had surgically repaired a compound fracture.   Surprisingly, her face remained unscathed from the ordeal.   Even in death, she was still beautiful.   The orderlies gently placed her on the slab.

"Thanks, guys," Nathan said with little enthusiasm.

Alpert and Newman gave him a tiny nod but were reluctant to speak as they rolled the stretcher from the morgue.   Nathan respectfully covered Tracy with a sheet up to her neck then studied her face.   Without an ounce of make-up, she still commanded attention.   Nathan frowned and shook his head as he leaned on the slab near her face.

"Oh, Dr. Kirby," he said softly.   "I never would have imagined you'd be here like this."   Nathan studied her a moment longer then gently brushed the hair from her face and sighed.   "Still as beautiful as ever."

Chapter Eleven

$\mathcal{I}$t was only a few minutes later when Rolan was seen pushing a stretcher along the empty hospital basement hallway. The wheels rolling along the concrete floor sounded like a freight train, breaking the silence. He had a distant look on his face and didn't appear pleased with his current task. He paused before the morgue and tapped on the door as he opened it. Rolan backed into the morgue with the stretcher then looked behind him. Tracy's sheet-covered body was still on the slab outside the freezer with her head still uncovered. It was an unexpected sight. Rolan looked around for Nathan then stared at Tracy's body. It was odd that she wasn't in the freezer. Perhaps odder still was seeing her head uncovered. It was strange Nathan would leave her like that. Nathan appeared from his office and looked surprised to see Rolan standing in the morgue with his stretcher.

"That was fast," Nathan announced. "They just brought her down a few minutes ago."

"I was wondering why she wasn't tucked away," Rolan said timidly while clearing his throat. "Sorry about showing up so early, but Lexx wanted to stop in and see Brandon." He shifted with discomfort. "I think when the call came from the hospital, she freaked a little about him. I thought it best to give her some time alone with him."

"Yes, of course," Nathan replied. "You could get some coffee while you wait. Although, I wouldn't advise getting it from the waiting room. Their coffee is terrible. As if waiting around in a hospital isn't bad enough; they could at least provide some decent coffee."

"Thanks, but I already had three cups," Rolan replied and noted Nathan's unhinged demeanor. He quickly brushed it off. "Lexx doesn't like me overly caffeinated. She says I'm too hyper as it is." He cocked his head to the side and gave the coroner a demanding look. "Can you believe that?"

Nathan managed a smile and snorted a soft laugh. "No, not at all."

✝

*O*t was later that morning at the Davenport Funeral Home. Lexx, who was standing inside the elevator, opened the old, gate-style door within the basement and backed out. She steered the stretcher containing the black body bag while Rolan pushed from the other end. Both wore matching frowns at their current task.

"I noticed Carson's car was gone," Rolan remarked with little enthusiasm.

"I know they only went out a couple times, but I think he really liked her," Lexx said with an added sigh. "It has to be hard on him knowing she's down here."

They pushed the stretcher toward the metal prep table. Lexx unzipped the body bag to reveal Tracy's corpse in the hospital gown. Both looked at her and frowned. Seeing her like that was indescribable.

"I'm a little bothered myself," Rolan replied gently, unable to take his eyes off the dead woman. "I mean, she was just here the other day looking so alive--"

"You need to separate yourself, Rolan. If you don't, you'll make yourself crazy."

"Too late. I've been crazy for years."

Lexx and Rolan transferred the deceased doctor's body from the stretcher to the metal prep table. Rolan moved the stretcher out of the way while Lexx untied the hospital gown. Rolan seemed uncomfortable and immediately fidgeted.

"Would it be weird if I took break during the wash prep?" Rolan asked.

Lexx eyed Rolan with surprise to his question. It wasn't like him to be tense around female clients. "A little," she remarked and tilted her head. "You've helped clean and sterilize female clients before."

"Yeah, but not one of Carson's girlfriends."

She could understand a little of what he was feeling, although it really wasn't an excuse. If he was that uncomfortable, she wasn't going to force him to assist in this case.

"You're excused this once," she announced then fidgeted herself. "But I may ask for a return on the favor."

Rolan stared at Lexx and slowly nodded with understanding. "If it comes to that, I'll take care of Brandon."

She didn't even want to think about it, but it was a relief. "Go on--get out of here."

As Rolan scurried from the room and up the stairs near the elevator, Lexx leaned on the prep table and stared at the once beautiful doctor now void of life. She took a deep breath, straightened, and removed the hospital gown.

†

*R*olan entered the kitchen from the basement and poured a cup of coffee. His excessive use of sugar and creamer defeated the purpose of coffee. He sat at the counter and opened the newspaper. There was a faint thump from the basement. Rolan lowered the paper and uncertainly looked to the basement door. Whatever he had heard wasn't a typical sound. He appeared curious and listened for further sounds.

"Rolan! Rolan!" Lexx was heard screaming from the prep room like a mad woman.

Rolan sprang up from the counter, his cup of coffee crashing to the floor, and ran for the nearby basement door. He thundered down the steps and bolted into the prep room. He nearly collided with Lexx, who had been hastily attempting to leave at the same time. She jumped back with surprise then held her head. She was visibly shaken.

"What is it? What happened?" Rolan gasped.

Lexx shook her head while trembling and hurried past Rolan to the nearby desk. She grabbed the cordless phone and pressed a button. Rolan looked at Tracy's lifeless, naked body lying on the prep table then looked back at Lexx with confusion. Whatever had happened was a mystery to him. Lexx was about ready to jump out of her skin as someone picked up on the other end.

"Yes, this is Lexx Davenport at Davenport Funeral Home," she said in rushed speech. "I need the police out here right away." There was a slight pause as she listened to the person on the other end. "No, I can't explain over the phone. Please send someone right away."

†

*L*exx leaned against the counter in the prep room with her head in her hands and remained distant and preoccupied. It had only been ten minutes since she hung up with the police, when Rolan was heard with the arriving officer. She could hear him on the steps speaking to the officer as they approached the prep room in the basement.

"I'd prefer if you spoke to Lexx," Rolan was heard saying to the officer.

Lexx straightened and attempted to collect herself as Hill entered behind Rolan. Hill glanced at the sheet-covered body then looked at Lexx. He was obviously bewildered and possibly losing patients with all the secretiveness.

"Will someone please tell me what's going on?" Hill finally demanded.

Lexx took a deep breath and tried to remain calm for the sheriff's sake. She knew he probably wouldn't handle the news very well.

"I started prep work on the client we'd just picked up--" She hesitated and was suddenly very uncomfortable explaining the situation to the handsome sheriff. It was an awkward conversation to begin with. "There's semen."

Hill stared at Lexx with a puzzled look and didn't quite understand the problem, although he did seem slightly uncomfortable with the current topic. Lexx groaned softly, hating to spell it out for him.

"It's a female client," she gently informed him.

Hill still appeared bewildered and raised a curious brow in question. "Okay--?"

Lexx shut her eyes, groaned softly, and then met his gaze with a look of dread in her eyes. "It happened postmortem."

Hill's expression suddenly dropped. That he understood. The world seemed to shatter around him, and he barely got the words out. "You mean--?"

She stared into his eyes with the answer clearly in her expression. "Yes, Sheriff."

Hill casually pointed across the room to the bathroom. "Is that a bathroom?"

Lexx nodded. Hill crossed the room in no particular hurry, entered the bathroom, and shut the door. Lexx and Rolan exchanged looks and waited for the sound both anticipated. Hill was heard heaving several times. The squeamish sheriff was about to have a very bad day.

Chapter Twelve

Hill aggressively paced the funeral home porch with his cell phone to his ear. He was about ready to jump out of his skin despite his calm tone with the person on the other end. Lexx and Rolan leaned against the railing and watched his endless pacing. Lexx thought his color seemed better now that he'd vomited, but his anxiety was rapidly increasing by the second.

"Yeah, I heard what you said, but it happened *at* the hospital," he said into the phone and started sounding agitated. "What's the protocol for that?" There was a long pause as the person responded to his question. "I know; I heard you say that too. You're not listening to me." There was another pause. "You're damned right I don't want to be the one to do that!" Hill groaned and continued his marathon pacing. "What I'm asking is who can I get to do it? Would the mortician be qualified--?" He was abruptly cut short by the person on the other end and instantly frowned in response to the comment from the other end. "No, *she's* not a suspect." There was another pause. His brows suddenly rose, and he seemed to get the answer he was looking for. "So a nurse or an *EMT* can do the test from a legal standpoint?" He awaited his final confirmation and appeared relieved while vigorously nodding. "Thank you! Thank you very much!"

Lexx and Rolan stared at him in silent question. He didn't respond to their looks. It was doubtful he even realized they were standing there by that point. Hill disconnected the call and immediately pressed another button. He finally stopped pacing, stood straight, and forced a smile as the call was answered.

"Monica?" he chirped a little too cheerfully. "I need a small favor--"

✝

*M*onica briskly entered the kitchen from the basement stairs while carrying a plastic bag. Her look conveyed her detest for everyone in the room. Lexx appeared from the basement stairs directly behind her with less emotion. Hill and Rolan stood by the kitchen counter and immediately jumped to attention as the two women approached. Monica handed Hill the plastic specimen bag while sneering at him.

"I'm never speaking to you again," Monica scoffed.

"Thanks, Monica," he said with an over exaggerated smile. "I love you."

"Prick--"

Monica left through the back, kitchen door, slamming it for added drama. Lexx leaned against the counter near Rolan and studied Hill.

"Your sister lacks that certain--" She considered her comment carefully then casually tilted her head while raising a devious brow. "--human quality."

"I don't know. I kind of like her," Rolan remarked while hiding his grin.

Lexx glared at Rolan. He fidgeted and attempted a more serious expression.

Hill exhaled deeply, glanced at the bag in his hand, and eyed both. "I don't want anyone touching that body until I get the report back on this sample," he informed them firmly.

"If I can't embalm her, I'll have to put her on ice," Lexx replied.

"That's fine," he said. "Just make sure no one else has access to her body. It's evidence."

"I think we need to get a drink," Rolan remarked. "Maybe two or three. I'll never understand why you don't keep hard liquor in the house."

"For the first time, I was wondering the same thing myself," Lexx announced then looked at Hill. "Sheriff? I'll bet you could use a drink."

"I'd love to get silly with you two, but I'm driving this to the city personally," he informed them. "I want this resolved as quickly as possible."

Hill left the house through the back door.

Rolan straightened and sighed. "Did you want me to push the doc into the freezer?"

"No, we won't be gone long. Just long enough to grab a bottle from the liquor store," she replied while holding her head. "We'll take care of her when we get back. Just make sure you lock the door behind us."

†

*I*t was only half an hour later when Lexx returned from her trip with Rolan to the liquor store. They hadn't even gotten one drink in when Carson pulled up and whisked Rolan away to help pick up another client. The sound of drinking alone wasn't appealing to Lexx, so she decided she should put Dr. Kirby in the freezer. She entered the basement prep room through the open door and was immediately puzzled. She knew she had closed the prep room door after she and Monica had gone upstairs. She took two steps into the room and suddenly stopped. All color drained from her face as her heart pounded roughly in her chest. She stared at the empty prep table containing only the sheet that had covered the corpse. Dr. Kirby's body was gone! Lexx felt fear shoot through her entire body, jolting her back to reality. She hurried to the large, walk-in freezer, opened it, and peered inside. She had hoped Carson had doubled back while they were gone and realized the body wasn't tucked away, but that was wishful thinking.

To her horror, the freezer was empty. Her anxiety was quickly rising to the thought of having lost a corpse. She looked back across the room, attempting to make sense of the situation, then had a terrible thought. She became alarmed and ran for her desk. Her day couldn't possibly get any worse. As she snatched the phone from its base, she knew Sheriff Burke's day wasn't about to get any better either. She pressed 911 with trembling hands and waited for someone to pick up. Her only saving grace was it was physically impossible for Sheriff Burke to respond to her missing corpse call, because he was undoubtedly on the road to the city. He'd be gone at least an hour roundtrip. She didn't want to explain to him how she possibly let this happen. A thought then occurred to her, sending terror through her. What would she tell Carson?

✝

It was nearly forty minutes after Lexx had called the police and insisted someone come out, offering limited explanation over the phone. She didn't need it getting around town that their funeral home lost a corpse. Lexx paced the porch for several minutes before she saw the sheriff's blazer flying up the funeral home driveway. Her heart nearly stopped when she saw it was Sheriff Burke behind the wheel. Wasn't he supposed to be driving that specimen to the city lab? She really didn't want to explain to him what she thought happened. Although the lights weren't flashing, she knew he broke a few speed laws on his way over. The vehicle came to a screeching halt just under the carport. Hill jumped out of the blazer and approached her with a concerned look on his face. He looked even worse now than he had earlier. She felt scolded before he even opened his mouth.

"Please tell me this is just a ploy to get me back, because you missed me," Hill announced firmly.

"Believe me, I wish it were."

Lexx hurried into the house. Hill hesitated and then followed her with less enthusiasm. They headed into the basement and looked around the empty prep room. Hill stood in the doorway to the open, walk-in freezer. He groaned and turned to face her with an expression that matched hers. Lexx leaned against the prep table and shifted uncomfortably.

"He was here, wasn't he?" she said with concern and insecurely rubbed her shoulders. "That bastard came in here and stole her body."

"You're sure you left her right here?"

"Rolan and I left right after you," she insisted. "I got back almost an hour ago. We were only gone thirty minutes at most. Carson pulled up right behind us, and Rolan went to the hospital morgue with him to pick up another client. I came down here to put her on ice, and she was gone."

Hill looked around and appeared frustrated with the entire situation. He looked back at her demandingly. "Was the door locked when you returned?"

"Upstairs? Yes, I had to unlock it when I got back," she replied.

"It didn't seem as if any of the main door locks had been jimmied," Hill remarked and shook his head. "I don't know how he would have gotten in."

Lexx considered the comment then suddenly frowned. "I think Carson told Nathan about the spare key so he could deliver a client once while we were away."

"Well, that's just great," Hill exploded and didn't know whether to pace or hit something. He finally looked at her. "Carson and Rolan don't know her body is gone?"

"No, I called you first," she replied then groaned softly. "That's not really a conversation I want to have with Carson. 'Oh, by the way, I lost a corpse'." Lexx groaned and held her head. "Carson is going to freak."

"Well, at least I won't be the only one."

"Is there any way we can keep this from getting out?" she asked while fidgeting and approached him. "Something like this could ruin our reputation."

"We have to report it," Hill informed her. "Unless he was stupid enough to hide her in the morgue freezer, it could take time to find her body. You won't be able to keep it from her family longer than a few hours."

"If he did steal her body, there are only so many places he could hide it in such little time." She considered her own comment. "What about the hospital incinerator?" she suddenly asked. "He has access to the incinerator. It could easily burn a body. Well, most of the body."

"Most?" He suddenly groaned and rolled his eyes. "Terrific," he muttered then eyed her sharply. "You and I are going on a little field trip. I'll pick up a warrant from the judge on the way to the hospital. If he did incinerate her body, you'll know what to look for."

She knew why he was dragging her along and decided to call him on it. "Come on, Sheriff, you just don't want to be the one looking through the morgue freezers," she remarked while heading for the prep room door.

Hill followed her toward the door. "Hey, this whole undead scene--it's all yours," he announced. "I arrest people. You play with dead things."

Lexx suddenly stopped before the door, turned abruptly, and glared at him. Her look alarmed him enough to cause him to take a quick step back. She sneered with irritation, turned, and left the prep room.

Hill frowned and muttered softly, "I'm going to pay for that comment."

Chapter Thirteen

It was early evening. The lab in the hospital's basement was bland and void of personality. It was obviously one of the less visited places within the hospital. The moderately sterile environment contained an exam table, a chair with one arm used to draw blood from patients, and a counter containing equipment used for checking blood work results. An older computer set on the counter alongside a microscope. Newman sat on the exam table while the hospital's phlebotomist, Frank, drew a blood sample from Newman's arm. Newman coughed several times and cleared his throat. He was unusually pale and sweating. The man in the lab coat remained focused on his work and didn't comment on Newman's condition. Gunther and a well-dressed, serious looking man in his late forties, Warren, entered the lab. Warren waited by the door while Gunther approached Newman on the exam table. He wasted little time checking the orderly's eyes with a penlight.

"Thanks for seeing me, Dr. Sharp," Newman said in a slightly raspy voice.

"What happened, Newman?" Gunther asked.

"I thought I was just catching something, but then I remembered what happened with Dr. Kirby," he announced and again cleared his throat. It was obvious talking was difficult. "Something had leaked from her lab coat pocket. I'm not sure what it was, but I started with a sore throat right after that. I didn't think about it at the time, but she may have taken one of your viles."

Gunther considered his comment then nodded. "Yes, I'd recovered the broken vile in the E.R., but that wouldn't make you sick," he explained while placing his hands in his lab coat pockets. "I created those serums to improve life. They help heal cells and tissue, particularly in the brain. That's why they're used on the patients with brain damage."

"Then why do all the patients keep dying?" Newman asked with concern.

"Those patients would have died without my injections," he explained and removed his cell phone that vibrated in his hand. He appeared disinterested in the caller and looked back at Newman. "If anything, the serum prolonged their lives. Once I find the right combination, it'll save lives."

Frank peered through the microscope from the nearby desk then looked at Gunther with an odd look of concern. "Take a look at his throat culture, Dr. Sharp."

Gunther approached Frank at the counter, set his cell phone down, and looked through the microscope. He hesitated with an expression of surprise then looked again.

"It can be transferred from saliva as well as blood contact," Frank informed him.

Gunther straightened and looked at him. "But you're sure it's not airborne?" he questioned then seemed less anxious. "That's a relief."

"Well, it's not airborne now," Frank remarked. 'It started out as a liquid then turned to gas, so initially it was airborne, but now it can only be spread by direct contact."

"Am I going to be okay?" Newman asked them from across the room and appeared concerned.

Gunther turned toward Newman on the exam table and showed little reaction. "It appears as if the serum is producing your flu like symptoms," he replied simply. "Thankfully, it's easily treatable, but anyone who came into contact with the vile when it broke will need to be treated or the flu will spread like wildfire." Gunther studied Newman, tilted his head, and appeared curious. "Who else was in the stairwell?"

"I didn't exactly stick around to see," Newman explained while again clearing his throat, "but I'm pretty sure it was that EMT guy and Rose from ICU."

"Yes, that's right," Gunther replied. "I met them in the E.R. What about Alpert?"

"No, I don't think so."

Gunther smiled reassuringly and gently patted Newman on the shoulder. "You just take it easy while I take care of that treatment for you."

"Thanks, Doc."

Gunther walked away from the exam table and approached the lab door where Warren waited. He gave him a nod then passed him for the door. Warren removed a gun with a silencer from his shoulder holster and shot Newman in the chest. Gunther left the room without stopping or looking back. Newman fell back onto the exam table with a thud. Frank casually looked from the dead man on the table to Warren, who replaced his gun to the shoulder holster beneath his jacket.

"I suppose I have to dispose of that," Frank announced without emotion.

Warren raised a skeptical brow. "Unless you'd prefer to administer *treatment* to the nurse and EMT."

"No, I have this," Frank announced with a dreary sigh while standing and approached the body on the exam table. "They're all yours. I wouldn't want to deprive you of your fun. I'll just need to get a stretcher from the morgue."

Frank casually covered Newman's body with a sheet and left the room with Warren. Gunther's cell phone left on the counter vibrated across the surface from an incoming call. A few minutes later, Frank returned to the lab with a stretcher and pushed it alongside the exam table with the sheet-covered body on it. He grunted while awkwardly attempting to transfer the body by himself. Once he moved Newman's body onto the stretcher, he noticed bright red blood had soaked through the sheet. Frank cursed softly and placed another sheet over the blood to conceal it. What he really needed was a body bag. There were usually old body bags next to the incinerator waiting to be burned. The incinerator room was at the other end of the hall near maintenance. It would be risky moving the body on the stretcher with blood soaking through for possible onlookers to notice. Although, at this time of evening, there wouldn't be anyone in the basement to notice. A quick trip to the incinerator room, and Newman's body would be disposed quickly and quietly. Gunther's cell phone again vibrated on the counter. Frank noticed the phone, approached, and picked it up.

"Yeah, Doc," he announced into the phone without waiting for a greeting. "You left your phone here. I'll leave it on the counter for you."

Frank set the phone down and turned toward the stretcher. Newman stood behind him with a glossed over look in his eyes and blood soaking the entire front of his shirt. Frank appeared horrified to see the dead man standing only a foot away from him. Before Frank could even gasp, Newman lunged for him and bit him on the neck. Frank thrashed and screamed while Newman pulled a large chunk of flesh from his neck. As Newman pulled back with the flesh in his teeth, Frank collapsed to the floor, clutching his bleeding neck, and gasped while dragging himself toward the door in a futile attempt to escape. Newman pounced on top of him and sank his teeth into his flailing arm. Frank weakly screamed as Newman tore flesh from his arm through the lab coat.

Chapter Fourteen

$\mathcal{T}$he elegant casket room within the funeral home had a variety of caskets on display varying in style and price to accommodate nearly every budget and taste. Some were plain and reasonably priced while others cost more than a brand new car. They were the Cadillac of caskets, as Carson liked to call them. Despite the purpose of the room, it was dressed with tapestries and curtains creating a soothing, relaxed atmosphere to simulate an eternal rest. Rolan and Carson pushed a covered stretcher into the room from the outer double doors beyond the driveway and toward the old, gate-style elevator. Rolan pressed the elevator button and turned to face Carson.

"I think I showed excellent restraint with Nathan," Rolan announced proudly.

"Yeah?" Carson scoffed while holding back his annoyance. "Well, part of me wished you'd taken his head off. One of us should have."

Both had their backs to the elevator as it was heard creeping up the shaft from the basement. It was old and made a terrible squeaking sound the last few years. It was long overdue for replacement, but Lexx loved it so much, they just kept repairing it time and time again.

"I'll take his head off next time," Rolan replied simply. "I promise."

The elevator stopped on their floor. Neither appeared enthusiastic enough to turn toward it. Their current conversation had them down. The door opened to reveal Tracy standing naked beyond the gate, although neither man turned to see her. Despite her gray complexion, numerous contusion, and abrasions, she was still quite beautiful. Carson opened the gate with his back to it and the dead woman.

His look was stern while staring at Rolan. "Her spirit won't rest until he's dealt with," Carson stated firmly. "She's going to have her revenge, I assure you."

Tracy stumbled out of the elevator on a severely broken ankle with her bone protruding from the torn incision. The crunch of bone alerted Rolan. He turned his head, saw her, and cried out with horror, frozen where he stood. Carson quickly turned, surprised by Rolan's look, saw Tracy directly behind him, and screamed in response. Tracy reached for Carson with her broken arm. Carson jumped backwards to avoid her hand and struck the stretcher. Tracy lunged forward, grabbed his head, and attempted to bite his neck as both crashed to the floor. Carson screamed and thrashed beneath Tracy while attempting to keep her from biting him. She snarled and snapped at his throat as he held her back.

"Get her off! Get her off!"

Rolan leaped past the stretcher and grabbed Tracy's arm. Her broken arm gave and the bone protruded through the skin. Rolan screamed with horror.

"I'm sorry! I'm sorry!" Rolan cried out.

Tracy turned her head and snapped her teeth at Rolan's hand clutching her arm. He released her arm and again screamed in terror.

"Do something!" Carson yelled while struggling against the woman on top of him.

Her attention again focused on tearing Carson's flesh from his body. She came at him with more vigor. He struggled to keep her from biting his face. Rolan stared at Tracy on top of Carson with horror in his eyes.

"I don't want to hurt her!"

"She's dead!" Carson suddenly cried out in panic. "Hurt her! Hurt her!"

Rolan grabbed Tracy around the waist from behind and hoisted her off Carson. He held her in the air while she growled and thrashed wildly against him. Several broken ribs now protruded from her side. Rolan cried out to the crunching of her ribs beneath his arms. Carson jumped to his feet.

"What do I do with her?" Rolan cried out.

"The casket!"

Rolan tossed her into the nearby, expensive casket. She landed inside the satin interior with a dull thud.

"Are you crazy? Not that one!" Carson cried out.

Tracy attempted to pull herself from the casket. Both men screamed. Without even thinking, Carson slammed the lid as she attempted to get out and caught her fingers. Two of her fingers broke off and fell to the floor with a creepy thud. Rolan screamed and leaped away from the severed fingers. Tracy pounded against the casket lid and nearly opened it. Both men jumped on the casket to keep it closed and panted heavily. She continued to thump from inside.

"What the fuck was that?" Carson exploded while staring at Rolan with his eyes bulging out of his head.

"How the hell am I supposed to know?" Roland cried out. "She's your girlfriend!"

"We need to find Lexx," Carson gasped while subconsciously running his fingers through his hair. "She'll know what to do. Let's lock this casket, so she can't get out."

✝

𝒢unther entered the hospital lab, heading straight for the counter containing his cell phone. His eyes strayed to the large amount of blood on the floor just before the counter. He stared with horror at a large streak of blood that traveled across the once white, sterile floor.

"What the hell--?"

Gunther nervously followed the blood trail with his eyes and looked past the open door. Frank was lying in a bloody heap in the corner of the room with his insides hollowed out and scattered organs on the floor surrounding him, apparently the parts Newman didn't like. Gunther gasped and quickly attempted to make sense of what he saw. He heard a gurgle alongside him. He slowly turned his head toward the door. Newman, who had been behind the door, now stood before him with Frank's blood seeping from his mouth, down his chin, and down the front of his clothing. Gunther cried out as Newman lunged for him. He attempted to push the dead man away from him. Newman bit his forearm while snarling savagely. Gunther pulled his arm back before he could tear out a chunk of flesh, but he had sustained a large, bleeding bite wound. Gunther clutched his bleeding arm, bolted from the room, and slammed the door behind him. Newman crashed into the door and pawed at it in vein with bloodstained hands for a few minutes. He looked back at Frank's body in the corner, lost interest in the door, and returned to the dead man in the corner. Newman sank his teeth into Frank's arm, pulling a large chunk of flesh from it, and chewed it savagely.

Chapter Fifteen

*W*arren sat on one of the benches smoking a cigarette just outside the emergency room door. He watched Evan and Monica as they refilled their emergency supplies within the ambulance across the parking lot. They had just returned from grabbing a bite to eat for dinner and appeared to be having a heated conversation. Actually, it seemed as if Monica was having a heated conversation while Evan did most of the listening.

"Can you believe the nerve of my brother?" Monica ranted to Evan, who was a little less enthusiastic with his work than usual. "I mean, who the hell asks someone to do something so twisted as a 'favor'?"

Monica seemed to move twice as fast at refilling supplies as her partner and practically did laps around him. Evan obviously wasn't feeling good and seemed to have little energy. It was hard to keep up with Monica most times as it was. Monica continued her rant and appeared unaware of Evan's listless condition.

"I tell you, I wish I'd been born an only child," she scoffed while tossing things from the bag and adding other items. "Maybe it's just me. Eight years in the Army and two tours in Iraq have a way of toughening a woman, I suppose."

"Let's not forget that little limo excursion from hell last year," Evan managed to tease.

She cast a glare at him. "Believe me," Monica muttered, "I've been trying to forget. How that man became a federal agent is beyond me."

Evan suddenly straightened and stared at his partner with surprise by her comment. "Seriously?" he demanded. "Four days in the backwoods of 'Deliverance' and a failed romance is all you have to complain about?"

She eyed him sharply. "Which part of two tours in Iraq were unclear, Evan?" Monica waved him off. "Four days in that dead village was like a field trip compared with all those months I'd spent in Iraq."

Evan leaned against the back of the ambulance, wiped the sweat from his forehead, and watched Monica continue to work. "Did your brother at least tell you why he needed you to do something so--" Evan hesitated and searched for a word.

"Icky?" she filled in the blank while raising a brow.

"Yeah, we'll go with icky."

"Of course he didn't," she snapped with a look of annoyance on her face. "He's secretive as usual." She frowned and shook her head. "God, he needs to get laid."

"You said he was with that girl at the funeral home," Evan remarked.

"Snow White?" Monica snorted a laugh and appeared humored. "I'm sure he'll die of old age long before he gets any from that one." She routed through the large emergency bag and looked disgusted. "We're nearly out of everything," she announced and finally looked at him. She stared at him as he sat on the tailgate and folded her arms across her chest with annoyance. "Please, by all means, rest. I'll carry your ass."

"I can't help it," Evan remarked while leaning his head against the ambulance doorframe. "I'm exhausted."

"You need to stop getting your freak on with Rose in the linen closet," Monica retorted. "You know you're completely worthless after getting your rocks off."

Evan managed a humored grin in response.

Monica shook her head at his amusement to her comment. "You either have zero stamina, or you're doing some seriously kinky shit in that closet."

"Wouldn't you like to know?" he teased.

She considered the comment only a moment. "Honestly, I would," Monica replied simply, "but if you disappointed me, I'd probably bitch slap you. I don't think our friendship can survive bad sex."

Evan chuckled.

"I'll get those supplies," she announced then walked away from him and toward the emergency room doors.

As Monica approached, Warren crushed his cigarette and walked past her in the direction of the ambulance. Evan remained seated just inside the back doors of the ambulance and rested his head against the side with his eyes closed. Warren removed his gloved hand from his pocket to reveal a syringe containing murky liquid. He kept it carefully hidden and glanced around the surrounding area for any onlookers. He was only a few feet from the resting paramedic when his cell phone rang. Warren suddenly stopped and reached into his pocket, but it was too late to silence his phone. Evan opened his eyes and looked at Warren. He had already returned the syringe to his pocket. Warren removed his cell phone and exchanged nods with Evan. He quickly turned and hurried away from the ambulance while placing the cell phone to his ear.

"I don't appreciate being interrupted," Warren snarled into the phone.

"Get back to my office right away," Gunther said while breathing heavily from the other end. It almost sounded as if he was running while talking.

"I wasn't quite finished--"

"Now, Warren!" The phone clicked.

Warren frowned and returned his phone to his pocket. He muttered something under his breath and headed back for the emergency room doors.

†

*G*unther ran into his office while breathing heavily and gasping for air. He had run the entire distance from the basement to his office on the fifth floor, taking the least traveled routes, which involved a lot of stairs. The surgeon wasn't in terrible shape, but he certainly wasn't in marathon condition. He found some gauze in a cabinet and wrapped his oozing, bleeding arm. The door opened, startling him. He pulled his lab coat sleeve down and turned to face Warren, who entered without care and appeared annoyed.

"Why did you interrupt me?" Warren demanded. "I was about to take care of our EMT situation."

"You can deal with them later," Gunther informed him while still panting out of breath. "That serum reanimated Newman. He came back to life and ate Frank."

"Ate Frank?" Warren asked with surprise and stared into Gunther's eyes, waiting for the punch line. When one didn't come, he eyed him skeptically. "What are you on?"

"Listen to me," Gunther shouted and took a quick step closer to Warren. He stared into his eyes with a serious look that surprised the tough man. "That serum reanimates the dead. Not just their tissue, but also their entire bodies. We need to dispose of Newman-- again."

"You're serious?" he announced and tilted his head. "You think he came back to life? Do you seriously believe Newman is a zombie?"

"You can have a look for yourself when you go back to the lab and shoot him again," Gunter lashed out. "We have bigger problems right now."

"Bigger than a dead cannibal?" Warren mocked.

Gunther was losing patience with the tough man standing before him. "If that serum was airborne in the stairwell when it affected Newman, that means it could have infected Dr. Kirby as well," he informed Warren. "If the funeral home embalms her and disposes her blood into the sewer system as many of them do, we could be looking at an epidemic of the entire town. I need you to find out what funeral home took her and bring her body back immediately." He attempted to compose himself and gingerly rubbed his wrapped arm beneath his lab coat. "Once I've done tests on her blood and tissue and confirm she hadn't been exposed, we'll burn all the bodies in the incinerator."

"What about the nurse and the EMT?"

"We have more than enough time to deal with them. Deal with Newman first, and then go to whichever funeral home the Kirby's contracted. Bring the doctor's body back here," he replied firmly then collected himself. He took a deep breath and calmed slightly. "I hope I'm being paranoid over nothing, but if I'm not and she's been infected, she could reanimate and do a lot of damage. I need to get this under control now."

Warren nodded despite his look of disbelief to what Dr. Sharp was saying and turned toward the office door.

"Warren," Gunther suddenly announced, causing Warren to turn and look back at the concerned doctor. "If she was infected and turned like Newman, there's no telling what she'll do and who she might injure. I'll need you to round up any witnesses and bring them to me. Understood?"

"And if they don't want to come willingly?"

"Then you have permission to bring them in any way and in any condition you feel necessary."

Warren gave him a slight smirk, nodded, and left the office. He obviously enjoyed his work a little more than he should. Gunther appeared concerned and rubbed the wrapped wound through his lab coat. The discolored blood was already seeping through his sleeve. It wasn't a good sign and infection was evident. Running a blood test on himself would tell him if the infection was life threatening or not. Unfortunately, the only place he could do a blood test was in the basement lab.

Chapter Sixteen

$\mathcal{I}$t was later that evening and the sun was finally setting over the quiet town. Monica sat within the back of the ambulance parked just outside the hospital emergency room. She busily worked on sterilizing the stretcher within the back beyond the open doors. Evan sat on the nearby bench and held his head with little movement. Normally he'd be smoking a cigarette, but he didn't seem to have enough energy to do even that. Monica glanced at him several times and became concerned about her partner. He no longer looked exhausted, he looked sick.

"Hey, you okay?" Monica finally asked.

"I feel like shit," he muttered. "I think I'm getting some crazy ass flu."

Monica jumped from the back of the ambulance, approached Evan while removing her gloves, and studied his pale, sweaty skin. She touched his forehead, expecting him to be burning up, and suddenly appeared surprised.

"Jesus, you're freezing," she gasped and allowed her concern to consume her. She wasn't exactly the most nurturing woman most of the time, but this was her partner and that made everything different.

"Let's get you into the emergency room and have one of the nurses look at you."

"I'm so weak," he said softly. "I can't believe how quickly this bug hit."

She reached down to help him up.

He held up his hand and protested slightly. "Don't get too close," he informed her in a faint tone. "I don't want you catching it from me."

Monica rolled her eyes and pulled him to his feet without hesitation. "Save your chivalric, sentimental bullshit for your girlfriend."

†

*T*he emergency room was only slightly busier than usual. There were a little over twenty people awaiting medical attention. A man and woman in their early thirties sat with a ten-year-old girl, Allison, who wore a torn, dirty dress. Her long, black hair contained fragments of dirt and tree bark. She held an ice pack to her lower arm. By the large amount of swelling and discoloration, her arm was undoubtedly broken. Her father, Peter, fidgeted with impatience from their wait. Her mother, Ellen, seemed more concerned over their daughter's discomfort.

"I don't know why you thought you could climb that tree, Allison," her mother gently announced while shaking her head with disapproval.

"The boys didn't think I could," Allison replied. "I knew I could, so I had to prove it."

"Yes, but not in a dress," her mother scolded.

Allison appeared ashamed and looked at her torn dress. "I'm sorry I ruined my dress."

Ellen laughed softly and gently hugged her daughter. "The dress can be replaced. It's you I'm worried about."

"It's okay, Mommy," Allison replied. "It doesn't really hurt that much now."

A robust woman in her early fifties, Pricilla, hurried across the waiting room and stopped before them with concern on her face. She stared at her granddaughter.

"What happened, my dear?" Pricilla asked.

Allison looked up and immediately smiled. "Nana!" The little girl sprang up from her chair and hugged her grandmother with her good arm.

She gently returned the hug and pulled away to look at her. "What did you do, Allison?"

"Showing off in front of the boys," Peter scoffed. "Where the hell are these people?"

He looked around the waiting room for any sign of a doctor, nurse, or orderly. None seemed to be available except Patty behind the desk. As if on cue, one of the nurses appeared from the coveted emergency room doors and approached them. She smiled pleasantly at Allison, although she seemed distracted.

"Let's take you back to one of our exam rooms and have a look at that arm," the nurse announced.

All three attempted to follow. The nurse looked back and maintained her polite demeanor.

"Just the parents, if you don't mind," she announced to the little girl's grandmother.

Pricilla managed a tiny smile, pretended not to be offended, and nodded. "I'll just wait here."

The nurse led Allison and her parents through the mysterious door to the emergency room. Monica helped Evan through the main doors and across the emergency room toward the front desk. Evan leaned on the front desk while Monica caught the attention of the older nurse busily working behind it.

"Patty, there's something wrong with Evan," Monica announced with mild concern in her voice. "He's got some sort of messed up flu, but there's no fever."

"Him too?" Patty asked and appeared puzzled. "There must be something going around. They brought Rose down from ICU, and Alpert collapsed a few minutes ago."

Monica's expression shattered and her mouth fell open slightly. "What?" she gasped softly then immediately tensed and attempted to mask her concern. "We all hang out together. That can't be a coincidence."

Patty appeared sympathetic as if she knew more than she led on. "Take him into room four. Dr. Sharp is on call, but for some reason he's not answering his pages."

Monica helped Evan through the double doors, down the hall to the end, and into exam room number four. She helped Evan onto the examination table. Despite sweating profusely, he remained cold. He immediately lay down with exhaustion. Monica found a blanket in a cupboard and covered him to help keep him warm. Evan caught her arm, surprising her. She looked into his eyes.

"You don't have to stay, Monica," he said softly. "If you want to check on--"

"I'm not leaving you until the doctor sees you, Evan," she stated firmly. "Stop being so stubborn."

"Maybe you should check on Rose for me and see if she's okay," he said gently then hesitated. "And, you know, Alpert, if you feel like it."

"I'll ask Dr. Sharp about their condition when he gets here," she informed him sternly. "Besides, you know Rose. She's probably telling Dr. Sharp what's wrong with her and what meds to prescribe." Monica snorted a laugh. "She's going to make a god-awful patient."

"Most nurses do," he softly teased.

Both heard Patty's page for Dr. Sharp over the intercom. Monica appeared puzzled then looked back at Evan while shaking her head.

"He's not exactly punctual, that one," she remarked. "If I'm ever sick, don't let him touch me. Something about him makes my skin crawl."

"You're not the first woman to say that," Evan replied softly while shivering beneath the blanket. "Rose can't stand him. She says it's his beady eyes."

"I don't know how she stands you," Monica snorted softly with a teasing smile at her partner. "You do realize that she's way out of your league."

Evan managed to chuckle softly. Monica looked at the open door and watched for the doctor. Her concern and hostility seemed to increase with each passing minute.

Chapter Seventeen

*T*he hospital's incinerator room was located in the basement at the opposite end of the building from the morgue. Lexx sifted through a pile of ashes in the massive incinerator with a special rake designed for such a task. Hill casually leaned against the wall and watched her work with a strange look on his face. She knew he was watching her, but she refused to acknowledge the attention. She knew that look, and it wasn't lust. It was that same look she'd seen on the faces of many men before. In their minds, she was some sort of science experiment gone astray. She hated that look. How could her Uncle Brandon not understand why she didn't date? He had to know what she dealt with every time she met a man with whom she was mildly interested. She often wondered if that was the same reason why he never married. Her thoughts were suddenly interrupted by Hill's thoughts spoken aloud.

"I don't get it," Hill said casually as he straightened while staring at her.

Lexx kept her attention focused on the piles of ashes. She was very aware that his comment wasn't about the task at hand, but she played dumb anyway.

"Get what?"

"Why would a young woman with so many options choose to be a mortician?" he finally asked the question she knew he'd been thinking the entire time.

Lexx glanced at him, appeared humored, and returned to sifting through the ashes. She had to admit; at least he asked it more tactfully then others had in the past. For a country cop, he wasn't as ignorant as most would think.

"Options?" she asked slyly. "Is that code for someone who's *not* hideously unappealing?"

He suddenly became uncomfortable and shifted awkwardly by her bluntness. "It just seems to me that your profession would hinder your social life."

Now he was just putting his foot in his mouth for her amusement. She couldn't resist teasing him, especially when he was obviously so uncomfortable with the topic he chose. Why did men like him make it so easy to torture them?

"Oh, you mean scare away shallow men who only see me as a sex object?" she asked then chuckled. "That's one of the few perks of my profession, Sheriff Burke."

He fidgeted from her comment. "I wasn't aware that made me shallow."

"I wasn't aware we were talking about you," she replied with some surprise.

"We weren't," Hill replied a little too quickly and continued to fidget.

She realized she'd embarrassed him, and, for once, it actually bothered her. She wasn't even sure why it bothered her. Lexx returned to sifting through the incinerator and considered the topic. Maybe he did just want to have an honest conversation and not poke fun at her profession.

"The funeral home has been in my family for generations," she announced as she worked. "My brother, Carson, was supposed to take the torch, but his fear of never getting laid was greater than his fear of corpses. So I dropped out of med school to get him off the hook and appease our parents."

"You wanted to be a doctor?"

"I thought I did," she replied.

"You shouldn't have put aside your dreams just to please your parents," he informed her. "Mine wanted me to be an Air Force fighter pilot." He considered his own admission and frowned. "I guess Monica was the son they'd always wanted."

"I'm sure your parents are proud of you too, after all, you're the sheriff."

"Honestly," he announced with a sigh, "at this point, all they want from me are grandkids. It's nice to know they think I'm good for something."

"God, they sound like my uncle," she remarked under her breath.

He continued to watch her half inside the incinerator. "So why don't you go back to med school and become a doctor?" he asked. "If it's what you want--"

"Don't be too shocked, Sheriff Burke. I actually like being a mortician." She grinned slyly and cast a devious look at him alongside her. "Freaking out former jocks like you is its own entertainment."

Lexx finally turned away from the incinerator and removed her gloves. "No human leftovers in there, although I did find quite a few rat bones."

"Rat bones?" he asked and grimaced.

"Yeah, it happens."

"That's nice," Hill muttered. Despite being sickened by the thought of charbroiled rats, Hill became defensive. "As much as I hate to deprive you the joy of mocking me, I wasn't a jock in school," he announced firmly. "I was the geeky kid who got picked on because his sister was cool and he wasn't."

"I lived in a funeral home," she announced while leaning her shoulder against the incinerator. "I was labeled creepy since I was five."

Hill offered a humored smile and chuckled softly. "You are creepy--"

Lexx shut the incinerator door with a little added vigor then glared at him. "Just for that, I'm not searching the morgue freezers for you." She walked past him for the door with her head held proudly.

Hill bolted after her and pushed the door closed while standing behind her, preventing her from leaving. She turned to face him with an annoyed glare. He placed his hands on the door on either side of her, stood uncomfortably close, and looked into her eyes. She wasn't sure she wanted him that close to her. Men, in her opinion, were odd creatures that couldn't be predicted. As she stared into his eyes, she hadn't realized they were that shade of blue. Almost ice blue. If she hadn't noticed how handsome he was before, she certainly noticed now.

"I meant that in a sexy, queen of the undead sort of way," he said in a voice that was beyond sexy.

His comment coupled with his closeness made her heart skip a beat and her pulse race slightly. She was suddenly reminded of how long it had been since she'd been in a man's arms. Rolan playfully hugging her didn't exactly count. For a brief moment, she wished he'd kiss her. A slightly dirtier scenario crossed her mind as well, but as always, that feeling passed quickly. She knew how charming men like Sheriff Burke operated. They only wanted one thing. Although it was a fine image to entertain, she wasn't playing along-- not today.

"Fine, you don't have to touch the bodies in the morgue," she scoffed and reluctantly gave in to his blue eyes. "You're almost as big a baby as Carson."

Lexx easily pushed him back, opened the door, and left the incinerator room. Hill groaned softly while watching her leave, ran his fingers through his hair, and then hurried after her.

Chapter Eighteen

Carson and Rolan leaned over the kitchen island counter with glasses of whiskey in their still trembling hands and the half-empty bottle between them. They'd put a serious dent in the 'just in case of emergency' bottle of whiskey Lexx had bought earlier that afternoon. Both men drank vigorously and in silence for nearly thirty minutes before either could speak about what had just happened. They were sedate and quite possibly drunk in a relatively short period of time.

"So what the hell are we supposed to do?" Rolan finally asked while glaring at Carson.

"We'll wait until Lexx gets back from her outing with the sheriff," Carson said in a slightly drunken tone. "She'll know what to do." He then muttered into his drink, "God, I hope she knows what to do."

"Do you think that's why she called him over in the first place?" Rolan asked while casting a quick glance at him. "That's what dispatch said, right? She called him? I mean, I don't think she called him to ask him on a date."

"If she saw Tracy like that, I'm sure she would have warned us," Carson bluntly informed him. "She wouldn't just leave something like that for us to blindly walk into." He then reconsidered the comment. "Me, maybe, but she'd never do something like that to you."

"Then why did she call the sheriff?" Rolan asked. "Where did they go?"

"Maybe he found some evidence on the DNA samples," Carson announced with a glimmer of hope. "We should call the hospital. Maybe they're there questioning Nathan."

"Hopefully the sheriff is arresting him as we speak," Rolan muttered.

There was a knock on the door, startling both. They simultaneously straightened, appeared alarmed, and stared at the back door as if it would bite them. For a brief moment, neither seemed able to move.

"Act casual," Carson finally announced as he collected himself and straightened his jacket.

"Act casual?" Rolan gasped with a look of horror on his face. "A dead, naked woman tried to bite me. Casual went out the door an hour ago."

Carson ignored the comment and approached the kitchen door. He looked out, appeared puzzled, and then opened the door to reveal Warren.

"Warren, Dr. Sharp's associate, right?" Carson asked and remained bewildered by the man at his door. "What brings you here at this hour?"

"There's a situation at the hospital," Warren casually informed him. "We need to return the corpse you signed out this morning immediately."

"Return?" Rolan gasped with horror. "Why would you need us to return a corpse?"

"There's an infection going around, and the corpse needs to be tested," Warren remarked with little emotion. "Have you started the embalming process?"

"Uh, no, we haven't," Carson replied while fidgeting and uncertainly cast a glance at Rolan.

Rolan was unable to do more than just stare at the man with his mouth hanging open.

"Good," Warren said and seemed moderately pleased with the response. "Let's get the body into your hearse and return it to the hospital."

"What sort of infection?" Carson questioned while tilting his head as he stared at Warren. "What exactly do you think the corpse is carrying?"

"I'm not at liberty to say, but it's urgent that we return the body immediately."

"Yeah, well, she may not want to go willingly," Rolan suddenly announced with a soft snort and took a large swallow of whiskey from his glass.

Warren eyed Rolan by the counter and appeared curious. "Did something happen?"

"Well, uh--" Carson fumbled and attempted to think of a reasonable explanation.

"She freaking tried to eat us!" Rolan proclaimed and nearly jumped out of his skin despite the large amount of alcohol in his system.

"There goes casual," Carson muttered.

The look they received from Warren was hard to read. He was a serious man and most found him intimidating. There was no telling what was going through his head.

"Did you contain her?" he suddenly asked.

Both men appeared stunned.

"You believe us?" Carson suddenly gasped while staring at Warren.

"Did you contain her?" Warren again asked in a more demanding tone. "Did she injure anyone?"

"Aside from jump-starting our hearts, no one was injured," Carson replied. "We secured her in one of the caskets and locked it for good measure."

"Where is the corpse?" Warren asked and looked around the kitchen.

Carson gave a slight nod to the room next door. "In the casket room. She's in the closed casket that sounds like a wild animal attempting to claw its way out."

Warren glared at Rolan. "You," he announced firmly, "pull the hearse around to the door." He then looked at Carson and pointed at him. "You, come with me."

As Warren headed into the casket room next door, Rolan and Carson exchanged concerned looks. It was troubling that the intimidating man actually believed their farfetched story. Who would believe such a thing? Warren had a reputation around the hospital, and it wasn't a good one. Something was definitely happening that neither of them wanted to know about.

†

Alison sat on the exam table within exam room six while her mother hovered over her with motherly concern. Her father checked out several items lying around within the small exam room. He'd already been through every cupboard and drawer, attempting to cure his boredom. He looked at his watch, groaned softly, and rolled his eyes.

"Why does this take so long?" he demanded and tossed one of the tools aside. "Can't they just take her for x-rays? Why all the waiting?"

"I'm sure they're busy," Ellen replied while sitting on the exam table with her daughter.

"The E.R. didn't look that busy," Peter scoffed and continued his pacing.

A lean man in a lab coat approached them. He was easily noticeable with his bleached blonde, spiked hair and many tattoos sticking out beneath his rolled lab coat sleeves. He smiled at Allison with boyish delight.

"I hear someone was climbing trees," Marco announced cheerfully. He looked at her arm and playfully gasped false surprise. "Oh, that looks like it smarts. How about we take you back for x-rays?"

"It's about time," Peter mumbled.

"Can we come along?" Ellen asked.

Marco looked at them and smiled sympathetically. "She won't be gone that long. You can't go into the room with her anyway," he replied. "I'll have her back in fifteen minutes. You can wait here, if you'd like."

They reluctantly agreed and watched as Marco helped their daughter off the table and led her from the room. Despite his slightly shocking appearance, she seemed particularly taken with him and happily walked alongside him.

"We're going to take a picture of your arm," he announced with enthusiasm as they headed through the door. "And if you stay real still for the picture, you get to pick out a ring from our treasure chest."

"Diamonds?" she asked with glee.

"Close," he replied cheerfully as they disappeared into the hallway. "They're rhinestones."

Peter shook his head and looked back at his wife. "Can we really trust that guy?"

"Why?" she suddenly asked.

"You saw the way he looked," Peter remarked while wrinkling his nose with distaste. "He looks like the sort of guy you'd find driving a windowless van."

"Peter--" she scolded.

Chapter Nineteen

*M*onica stood alongside Evan's examination table in exam room four. She now wore a surgical mask and latex gloves as an added precaution to his unidentified illness. Evan was completely pale, drenched in sweat, and trembled from his cold chills. Monica attempted to keep him covered and warm. Her concern won over her annoyance with the doctor, who still hadn't bothered to check on them. It seemed odd that even the nurses hadn't checked on them. There had been several emergency pages for both the doctor and orderlies to one of the rooms, but that wasn't uncommon in an emergency room. Monica wiped the cold sweat from Evan's forehead with a cloth and attempted to soothe him despite her annoyance with the hospital staff. He clung to the blanket and shivered uncontrollably.

"Hey, it's going to be okay, Evan," Monica said in her best sympathetic tone. She uncertainly looked around and again allowed her irritation to surface. She looked back at him and tried to control her hostility. "You just keep warm. I'm going to find that damned doctor myself."

"Don't beat anyone up on my account," he said weakly then attempted a grin.

Monica removed her mask, returned the knowing smile, and gently squeezed his shoulder. "If I beat up anyone, you know it's for my own pleasure," she teased him gently although the slight snarl in her voice conveyed her seriousness.

Evan took pleasure in her anger even in his weakened condition. She tossed her mask aside and stormed from the room while ripping off her latex gloves. Monica entered the corridor and immediately looked around. The corridor seemed oddly empty considering all the earlier emergency pages. There was a commotion coming from one of the exam rooms further down the hall. Several nurses and orderlies suddenly appeared as if out of nowhere and ran to exam room one. Monica appeared curious, picked up her pace, and hurried after them. She entered the exam room in time to witness Alpert being tackled by several orderlies while a nurse tried to give him a sedation injection. A second nurse lie on the floor clutching her bleeding neck as a third nurse attempted to control the nurse's bleeding.

Alpert had blood down his chin and the front of his scrub uniform, but there didn't appear to be an open wound to cause so much blood. He bit one of the orderlies on the arm as another nurse injected him with the needle. Monica stared helplessly as Alpert tore flesh from the orderlies arm. The nurse on the floor began convulsing as she bled out. Monica eyes widened with horror at the thrashing nurse almost certainly bleeding to death. She wasted little time grabbing a box of gauze pads and dived to the floor alongside them.

"Pinch the artery!" Monica cried out while attempting to assist the nurse.

Alpert suddenly broke free from the bleeding orderly and bit him on the shoulder. As the bitten orderly pulled away from Alpert, he stumbled backwards into Monica, who was crouched on the floor, and knocked her the rest of the way to the floor with him. Monica scrambled out from beneath the fallen orderly and flipped onto her backside. The nurse who had bled out on the floor suddenly grabbed the nurse assisting her, sank her teeth into her neck, and ripped a large chunk of flesh from her neck. The nurse screamed while attempting to fight her off. Monica leaped to her feet and stared at the startling scene with horror on her face. Alpert suddenly looked at Monica. She caught his gaze, stared into his lifeless eyes, and then looked at the blood running down his chin to his blood-soaked scrub top. She couldn't move and only stared helplessly. Alpert snarled at her through bloodstained teeth.

†

90

*W*ithin exam room six, Peter paced the length of the room and looked out the open doorway several times. Ellen sat on the exam table and attempted a calm attitude, although she was failing miserably. She'd flipped through the same magazine three times without reading a single article.

"It's been over half an hour," Peter announced and looked back at his wife sitting on the exam table with her magazine. "What's taking them so long?"

"I guess they're busy today," she gently replied even though she showed signs of concern as well.

Peter was hostile enough for both of them. "I told you I didn't trust that guy," he announced sternly while pointing a demanding finger at her. "We should find someone and demand to know where they took our daughter."

Patty hurried past the exam room. Peter immediately stepped into the hall and caught her arm, startling the older woman. She turned to face him.

"A man from x-ray took our daughter over half an hour ago, and they're not back yet," Peter informed her as his temper rose with his blood pressure.

"They were calling for assistance with an emergency," Patty announced as she removed a folder from the wall near the door. She seemed preoccupied but did her best to cover. "Personnel in x-ray may have reported to the emergency." She flipped through the file while entering the exam room with them. She looked over the file and nodded. "X-ray to rule out fracture of the lower, left arm," she announced. "I'm sure she's probably still in x-ray." Patty looked back at Peter. "I just have to check on that emergency page, and then I'll locate your daughter."

Another nurse appeared in the open doorway behind Patty. Peter saw the nurse and sighed with relief.

"Well, it's about time--" he announced and took a step toward her.

He suddenly stopped and stared at her with surprise. Rose stood in the doorway with blood spattered across her once white uniform. There was blood seeping from her mouth and down her chin.

"What the hell--?" Peter gasped.

Patty turned to see Rose standing just behind her. She gasped with surprise to the young nurse's condition and took a quick step toward her.

"Rose, what on earth happened--?"

Rose suddenly snarled, exposing bloodstained teeth, and lunged for Patty. She tackled the older nurse into the exam table, knocking Ellen to the floor. Rose bit into the flesh on Patty's face while the older nurse screamed and thrashed against her. Ellen remained on the floor and watched in horror as the flesh was torn from the nurse's face. Peter took a step back while staring with a look of shock. Ellen sprang to her feet. Rose lunged for Ellen, knocking her against the counter. Several items fell from the counter with a crash. Ellen attempted to hold Rose back to keep her bloodied teeth from her face. She stared with horror as the chunk of flesh fell from Rose's mouth.

"Peter, do something!" Ellen screamed while struggling with the aggressive dead woman.

Peter looked from Patty clinging to her bleeding cheek while leaning on the exam table to his wife attempting to hold back the zombie nurse. He suddenly turned and ran from the room.

"Peter!"

Patty stumbled across the exam room, removed a scalpel from one of the drawers, and stabbed Rose in the back of the neck. Rose released Ellen and spun toward Patty. She again lunged for Patty. Patty screamed and stabbed her in the throat with the scalpel. The sharpened blade plunging into her neck didn't even faze the snarling nurse. Ellen removed a metal tray from the table, tossing all the tools from it as she coiled back, and swung for Rose's head. The metal tray made a loud, metallic clang against the back of her head, denting the tray. Rose was knocked off balance. Ellen grabbed Patty's hand and pulled her from the room, slamming the door on Rose behind them.

Patty and Ellen ran down the hallway toward exam room one and the sounds of life, hoping to find help. They heard a shrill scream coming from the room and immediately stopped. There was a snarling sound behind them. Both looked back. Rose stood in the hallway with her sights on them. Patty and Ellen stared at her with horror. Rose ran for them.

"The doctor's lounge!" Patty cried out and pointed just ahead of them.

They ran for the closed lounge door not far from them. Rose suddenly tackled Patty and drove her into the wall alongside the doctor's lounge doorway. As Patty's head struck the wall, the sound of the bones in her neck snapping was almost deafening. Patty fell to the floor with Rose on top of her. Rose tore into the back of her neck with her teeth, tearing a large chunk of flesh. Ellen stared in horror, but it was obvious the older nurse was dead.   Ellen darted into the doctor's lounge and slammed the door behind her.

Chapter Twenty

*M*onica stared at the dead look in Alpert's eyes as he stood in the exam room doorway with his eyes locked on her. He suddenly snarled, charged for her, and tackled her to the floor. Monica reacted without thinking, grabbed his scrub shirt as he knocked her down, and, using his momentum, flipped him over her as they hit the floor. She rolled into a crouched position, grabbed her cell phone, and pressed a button as she sprang to her feet. The emergency dispatch could barely be heard above the commotion within the exam room.

"This is Sheriff Burke's sister," she shouted into the phone. "I'm at the hospital! They're killing one another! You need to send help!"

The third nurse was now on her feet and tore into the second nurse's lower arm with her teeth. The woman screamed with surprise and agony while attempting to pull her arm free. She thrashed and punched the nurse to no avail. As Monica assessed how to help the screaming nurse, Alpert returned to his feet with his sights again on her. Monica stared into his dead eyes and appeared horrified as he bared his bloodstained teeth. She no longer knew this man, and he intended to kill her.

"Oh, shit!" Monica gasped.

She bolted from the room with Alpert chasing her. Monica ran through the now bustling corridor and the scene of mass chaos as an infected Rose ran down the hall chasing staff and patients. A man was seen just ahead running into the x-ray waiting room. He turned while closing the door. It was Peter. Monica frantically waved to him as she ran.

"Wait!"

Despite seeing her running for him and the door, Peter shut the door. Monica slammed into the door and attempted to open it. It was locked! She pounded on the door while screaming profanities at the man staring at her from the glass on the other side. He wasn't malicious; he was just too scared to let her inside. Monica kicked the door then turned just in time to see Alpert nearly on top of her. Monica dodged beneath his grasping arms, allowing him to strike the door. Peter jumped away from the glass on the other side, startled by the orderly's impact against it. Monica ran in the opposite direction and witnessed nearly a dozen infected people tearing into their screaming victims. A quick assessment of the situation indicated there was nothing she could do for any of them. Rose, with blood now running down her chin and shirt, saw Monica sprinting through the corridor and ran for her. She had Rose approaching from the front, and Alpert only a few feet behind her. Monica threw herself to the floor and slid on her right hip past the zombie nurse, allowing Rose to crash into a nearby wall. Alpert was nearly on top of her now. Monica sprang to her feet and shoved a stretcher into her infected friend. It only briefly slowed him down.

Rose regained her balance and attacked a man attempting to flee another infected nurse. She took him to the floor, and he was immediately piled upon by several infected people. By the sounds coming from the man under the pileup, they were tearing him apart. Monica continued to run along the hall with Alpert in hot pursuit. She bolted into exam room four and slammed the door shut. Alpert struck the door and thumped against it with his body while snarling like a wild animal. Monica flipped the lock on the door and stared out the small window. Alpert pounded his head against the window, streaking it with blood while attempting to get to her. Monica jumped back with surprise and stared at him with the horror evident on her face. She clutched her head and took a deep, shaken breath. For a brief moment, it almost appeared as if she were about to cry. She collected herself and turned toward the exam table. Evan was now on his feet and clung to the counter with his head hanging down. Monica straightened with a renewed sense of purpose and newly founded anger.

"I'm going to get us out of here," she announced firmly as she approached. "We can make it to the ambulance. It's parked right outside the emergency room door. I just need a minute to think--"

Evan lifted his head and slowly looked at her. He exposed his teeth as bloody drool ran down his chin and had that same dead look in his eyes she'd seen in Alpert's eyes. Monica stopped midstride and stared with horror at her infected partner. He snarled and lunged for her. Monica cried out and attempted to bolt from his path. Just outside the door, Alpert slammed his face against the window and clawed at the exam room door. Monica screamed from inside. A crash followed and the thick door vibrated with a dull thud. Monica's screams subsided. A wounded nurse screamed and ran with a limp past Alpert down the hall. Alpert saw his lumbering meal run past him and pursued her. On the floor beneath the exam room door, blood rapidly spilled out from under it.

†

*P*eter cowered within the x-ray waiting room and slowly backed away from the door. He stared at the zombies piling against the thick window. They pawed at the glass with blood-covered hands and attempted to reach him. The glass and door were thick enough that there was little chance they'd break through. The terrified screams of men and women being torn apart by the infected echoed into the x-ray waiting room. What should have subsided as the flesh was torn from their bodies didn't end their screams. Peter's shoulders sagged as he sobbed only a moment. He looked around the x-ray waiting room. It was empty with no other sounds. He saw the phone on the desk just beyond the sliding glass window in the nurse's station. He ran around to the side door and entered the station.

Several chairs were overturned, but there wasn't any blood, suggesting whoever had been attacked had escaped. Peter grabbed the phone on the desk and pressed buttons, unable to figure out how to get an outside line. There was a faint thump from nearby. He uncertainly turned and looked around. The room was empty. Peter returned to the phone and continued pressing the numbers in different sequences in order to get an outside line. A hand appeared from beneath the desk and grabbed his leg. He cried out and leaped away from the desk. A nurse in her late thirties crawled out from under the desk.

"You have to press nine for an outside line," she told him while flustered and out of breath.

He saw her, exhaled deeply, and relaxed. "Damn it," he gasped softly. "You scared me."

As she straightened, he saw her ankle was in a cast. "Human nature," she informed him. "Fight or flight, right? Well, sometimes we hide when we can't do either of those."

"I hear you," he replied as he pressed nine then dialed 911. "We just need to ride it out and let the police or the goddamned National Guard end all this." He glanced at the nurse and waited for someone to answer his call. "I think we're safe in here. The doors and windows are thick."

No one was answering the emergency line. Peter became disgusted and slammed down the phone. They heard a low gurgle from nearby. Both looked across the room to the open nurse's station doorway. Marco, the tattooed x-ray technician, stood in the doorway while holding what appeared to be a woman's scalp containing long, dark hair. Both stood frozen and stared at the zombie technician still in his protective gown.

"That's the technician who brought my daughter back here for x-rays," Peter gasped then stared at the scalp with horror. "Oh, God, is that my daughter's hair?"

"What do we do?" the nurse asked softly.

Peter considered their options only a moment while briefly looking around. "Through the window and into the waiting room," he replied in a soft tone. "Once we're out, I'll run around and lock that thing in here."

The zombie technician took a step toward them while tossing the scalp to the floor. It made a grotesque splattering sound as it hit the floor. The nurse nodded in response while staring at her zombie co-worker.

"Remember flight or fight?" she asked Peter without taking her eyes off the zombie in the protective gown.

"Yeah," he replied and stared as well. "Do you have a better idea?"

"Yes, I do," she replied softly.

The nurse suddenly shoved him with all her force in the direction of the zombie technician. Peter was able to stop his forward motion before being propelled into Marco. As he attempted to jump back, Marco leaped on top of him and tore into his shoulder. He screamed in terror and pain while attempting to tear the zombie off his shoulder. As he shoved Marco away, he looked across the nurse's station to see the nurse climbing through the window despite her leg in a cast. He sneered and chased after her. She shut the window and wedged something between the glass to keep him from opening it. As he turned for the door, Marco again jumped on top of him. He held his arm out to stop the assault. The zombie bit into his arm and tore a chunk of flesh from Peter as he screamed. The amount of blood was staggering. Peter was finally able to shove the zombie back, darted past it, and ran for the open nurse's station door only a few feet away.

The nurse stood just outside the door and slammed it shut. He attempted to open it, but she braced herself against the door to keep him from getting out. There was a snarl behind him. He quickly turned. Marco lunged for him, knocked him against the door, and ripped the flesh from his neck. The nurse remained braced against the door from the opposite side as the man screamed and the door thumped against her body. There was fight or flight; and then there was survival. She was ensuring hers.

Chapter Twenty-one

*P*ricilla sat in the E.R. waiting room with a magazine on her lap, which she flipped through with little interest. She glanced at her watch, set the magazine aside, and looked around the waiting room. There weren't any nurses or orderlies anywhere. Even the older nurse behind the front desk was conspicuously missing. Several emergency pages had caught the attention of the fifteen or more people still awaiting word on loved ones or treatment within the waiting room. The emergency pages had subsided nearly forty minutes ago, and they hadn't seen anyone since. The commotion within the emergency room beyond the double doors was unusually loud, indicating they had a trauma case of some sort requiring all personnel. Oddly enough, there hadn't been any ambulances or EMT's floating through for nearly an hour. Pricilla finally stood, stretched her legs, and approached the front desk. She looked behind the desk, but there wasn't anyone in the back area either. The others still within the waiting room were becoming equally restless from their unusually long wait.

Emmerich wasn't a big city. Their hospital didn't usually have long waits. Something seemed wrong. The sound of the double doors was finally heard opening for the first time in almost an hour.

Pricilla glanced at the doors along with several others, eager to be called next. An orderly, based on his scrub uniform, stood in the partially open doorway. Since it wasn't a nurse, nearly everyone returned to their magazines or entertainment on their cell phones. It seemed odd when one person within the waiting room suddenly let out a slight gasp and stood abruptly. The parting of air behind Pricilla caused her to turn toward the desk. Patty stood behind the front desk only a foot away from Pricilla. The flesh from the left side of her face was almost completely gone, leaving her eye dangling from the bony socket, and exposing the upper half of her jaw. She snarled with bloodstained teeth and lunged for Pricilla. Pricilla suddenly cried out. There were several screams matching hers within the waiting room. Pricilla leaped out of the lunging zombie nurse's path. Patty struck the tall desk and narrowly missed grabbing the grandmother with her blood covered hands. Pricilla turned to run and warn the others, but it was already too late.

Alpert was within the waiting room and tore out the throat of a thrashing woman in his arms. One of the men within the waiting room punched him in the back of the head and the kidneys until he released the woman. The woman clutched her bleeding throat as blood poured past her hands and down her chest. Alpert spun to face the man with a large chunk of the woman's throat still between his teeth. As he snarled and lunged for the man, the flesh fell from his mouth. The man appeared horrified at the grotesque image and jumped backwards, out of his path. He collided with Rose behind him, who clutched his face and shoulder while sinking her teeth into the side of his neck. He attempted to pull away from her while screaming, but she remained glued to him, shredding the skin on his face with her fingernails until they reached his eye. Her fingers dug into his eye socket, blood spraying everywhere as he thrashed and screamed.

Everyone screamed and sprang to their feet from the initial, bloodcurdling scream. When they saw the bloody scene unfolding, several people ran for the main door to escape. Three of them made it through the door. Alpert tackled a fourth man into the door, stopping the stampede in their tracks. Pricilla backed away from Patty and the doors while watching helplessly as Alpert aggressively tore the flesh from the man's face with his teeth. There were more screams as a few more zombies stumbled through the inner doors into the waiting room, leaving the main entrance and the exam area doors blocked with ravenous undead. As the zombies stormed the waiting room, patients and visitors screamed and ran despite having no place to go. Pricilla watched a moment longer as if unable to move.

Sheer panic was driving the masses and any rational thought seemed to dissipate. Patty again attempted to reach for Pricilla, but couldn't make it past the counter height desk. Pricilla snapped out of her daze, grabbed a nearby chair, and slid it in front of the counter. She grabbed a discarded crutch leaning against the wall near several wheelchairs and swung for Patty's head.

As the crutch connected with Patty's head, her already broken neck gave, throwing her head unnaturally sideways and onto her shoulder. Despite her head resting on her shoulder, she still snarled at Pricilla. The older woman took several steps back then ran for the desk and rammed the crutch into Patty's chest using her forward momentum. Patty was thrown backwards several feet and crashed into a large filing cabinet. Pricilla jumped on the chair and looked across the chaotic waiting room as several others were knocked to the floor by the flood of zombies. Anyone falling to the floor was immediately piled upon, sealing their fate as zombie fodder.

"This way!" Pricilla cried out to anyone who could hear her while waving her hands.

As she climbed on top of the desk, several others ran for her. She wasn't an agile woman anymore, but she managed to climb from the higher counter down to the lower desk and onto the floor without falling. Several men and women climbed over the desk, some using the chair and others haphazardly scrambling over the counter. One man stopped to help a woman onto the desk, and he was grabbed by the zombie directly behind her. She screamed as the man was pulled to the floor and piled upon by several more zombies. He vanished beneath the pileup of zombies and only his screams indicated what became of him. Another man pulled the startled woman from the desk to the safety of the other side. Pricilla led the charge from the front desk and into the back exam area. She suddenly stopped and was nearly toppled by those directly behind her. Within the emergency room corridor, several zombies fed on those less fortunate. Other zombies attempting to pass through the emergency room doors saw them and immediately backtracked. Pricilla and her six followers were running out of options. Patty was heard snarling behind them, her awkwardly placed head lying on her shoulder.

"Over here!" shouted a familiar female voice from further away. "Mom, over here!"

Pricilla looked down the hall past several zombies on the floor and on a slower approach for them. Ellen stood inside the doctor's lounge doorway waving her arms to her mother. It was crazy, but that wasn't going to stop a mother from reaching her daughter.

Pricilla charged down the corridor as fast as her fifty-five year old legs would carry her. All six men and women followed in a stampede relying on the herd mentality. Several zombies lunged for Pricilla in the lead. The older woman turned into a Roman warrior and swung her crutch like a sword at each zombie within striking distance all while never slowing. She took down four zombies and plowed straight through the fifth. Several zombies chased after the small herd of humans that were their meal. Pricilla ran through the open door as her daughter stood aside, giving room. Five of the six made it through. The sixth, a woman, was tackled into the nearby wall by one of the faster moving zombies. She was slightly dazed as the zombie's teeth came at her. She screamed and attempted to hold the ravenous undead back, giving it opportunity to bit her lower arm. She screamed as its teeth punctured her skin. It was about ready to rip her flesh when the broad end of a crutch struck it in the face. The zombie flew backwards and struck the floor. Pricilla pulled the bleeding woman into the room and sneered at the zombie on the floor. She slammed the lounge door.

Chapter Twenty-two

The hearse pulled up to the hospital and stopped short of the parking lot. There were people running around the area surrounding the main entrance to the hospital in a state of mass chaos. CDC and state police surrounded the front of the building with flashing lights and vehicles blocking the entire front entrance. The screaming, panicking people were detained by the police and CDC. No one was allowed to leave. The only people attempting to get closer were the flocking reporters freshly arriving on the scene. Men in biohazard suits checked over those outside while the police kept everyone rounded up, keeping the press away with a wall of emergency vehicles. Rolan sat behind the wheel of the hearse and watched the mass hysteria surrounding the once quiet hospital. Warren sat in the passenger seat and stared out the hearse's windshield, looking equally surprised.

"They're sealing the doors," Warren suddenly announced, showing panic for the first time. "We need to get the doctor inside before the building is completely sealed."

Carson poked his head out front from the back. "That's a bad idea."

"It's possible she's patient zero," Warren announced sternly. "In case you don't understand what that means, she could hold the cure for all this." He glared at Carson just behind him. "We have to get her inside."

"Wouldn't it be beneficial to hand her over to the CDC?" Rolan asked. "They'd know what to do."

"Dr. Sharp is the only one who can stop this," Warren informed him. "We need to take her to him. CDC won't know what they're looking for, and they'll waste a lot of time with unnecessary tests." He casually pointed around back. "There's the rear entrance to the basement. They may not have gotten to it yet. It's easily overlooked."

"And then we're also stuck inside," Carson informed him with panic in his voice.

"If we can stop it, that won't matter," Warren said as he became agitated. His look was stern, alarming Rolan. "Drive around back."

†

Lexx and Hill entered the silent, empty morgue and looked around. There was no one around. Nathan possibly went home for the evening, leaving them alone with the freezers and empty exam tables. Hill approached the office and peered inside. He looked back at Lexx and casually placed his hands on his holster.

"I guess your boyfriend went home for the evening," Hill announced.

She glared at him. "That's not funny."

Lexx approached the freezers and opened each. Nearly half were empty. The others contained the recently dead crash victims. Most hadn't been picked up for their final arrangements. As Lexx checked toe tags and uncovered each body, she frowned with disgust. She couldn't believe how many of the critical crash victims had died in the last two days. She opened another door containing a sheet-covered corpse. Nathan entered, startling both, and appeared surprised to see Lexx standing before the sheet-covered corpse on the metal tray. He gave her an odd, quizzical look.

"Lexx, what's going on?" Nathan asked then glanced at Hill on the other side of the room.

Hill turned official, approached Nathan, and showed him the search warrant. "We have a warrant to search the hospital for a missing body."

Nathan wasn't impressed by Hill's professional attitude, but was surprised by the comment. "Missing body?" he asked. "What missing body?"

"Dr. Tracy Kirby," Hill replied.

Nathan appeared surprised and looked at Lexx, who pulled the sheet back to reveal another crash victim. "You lost Dr. Kirby's body?"

Lexx didn't even acknowledge his scathing question. She had limited patients with the man she idolized for years. She didn't even want to look at him, but she couldn't avoid it after noticing another crash victim. Lexx stared at him with the surprise evident on her face.

"Four of these bodies are victims from the crash, Nathan," she suddenly announced. "That means nearly everyone in ICU from the wreck died in the last two days."

Nathan nodded. "That's correct," he replied. "About Dr. Kirby--"

"I saw Dr. Sharp injecting something into my uncle's IV, and it wasn't listed," Lexx informed him. Her concerns were stronger than her repulsion for her former friend.

The coroner appeared surprised and stared at her. "Why would a surgeon be administering medication?" he demanded. "That's the nurse's job."

"Exactly," Lexx announced and felt her anger welling inside her. "Dr. Kirby was going to look into it for me. Maybe she found something she shouldn't have." She felt the hairs on the back of her neck stand on end to the thoughts she was thinking. "If I could see her file, I could tell what angle she hit the steps."

"You don't need her files," Nathan replied. "I'm almost certain she went backwards down the stairs with no indication she attempted to brace her fall."

Hill looked from Lexx to Nathan and appeared surprised. "Are you saying you both think she may have been pushed or thrown down the stairs?" he suddenly asked.

Both nodded.

"Her file should be archived in the file room down the hall," Nathan informed him.

"We wouldn't need a warrant if you have access to those files," Hill pointed out.

"Give me ten minutes," Nathan replied then removed a set of keys from the wall and left the room.

Lexx slid the body back into the drawer and moved to the last freezer door while casting a look at Hill. "We're going to need tox screens on all the crash victims who died as well as my uncle and Ava Martin," she sternly announced as she opened the freezer door. She looked at the toe tag on the dead body and immediately frowned. Lexx looked at Hill and raised a brow. "It's Ava Martin," she said with disgust. "That means my uncle is the only one left." She slammed the freezer door with disgust. "If Dr. Sharp was injecting them with something questionable, there's a good chance my uncle will die too."

Hill studied her hostile expression and attempted to soothe her mood. "You don't know that."

Lexx again opened the freezer door and pulled out the slab containing Ava Martin. She pulled the sheet back to reveal the young woman wearing a hospital gown. As she stared at the partially frozen body, she couldn't help but be disgusted by the situation and more than concerned for her uncle's fate. Hill stared at the dead woman and grimaced. He fidgeted and attempted to look anywhere but at the corpse. Lexx wasn't sure if she found his squeamishness around the dead off-putting or endearing.

"She's not going to bite you, Sheriff."

"I know," he muttered, again fidgeted, and then looked at Lexx. "Aren't you even the least bit freaked that they might sit up or open their eyes?"

She grinned and had to keep from laughing. "Believe me, it's happened."

He appeared stunned. "You mean a corpse actually sat up once in front of you?"

"It's just muscle spasms and reflexes," she informed him.

Hill groaned softly and again looked away. "Nice to know," he muttered.

"Keeping their eyes closed is more difficult than you'd think. We need to use these--"

"I don't really need to know," he announced gruffly.

Lexx hid her smirk.

He finally looked back at her and appeared curious. "Can you do blood work?"

"No," she replied and finally looked at him, "but Nathan does tox screens as part of his job. He can make that decision without anyone's permission."

"The man also abused a corpse," Hill reminded her. "Do we really want his help?"

Lexx frowned while staring at him. She felt defeated with the response she had to give him. "It'd be the proof you need to get a court order to check the other bodies."

"It would make my job easier," he replied with a defeated sigh then ran his fingers through his black hair. He again looked at the dead woman on the slab. "Could you--?" Hill made a motion for her to push the slab back inside the drawer.

"Honestly, Sheriff," she said with a groan and placed the sheet back over Ava.

Chapter Twenty-three

The hospital waiting room was strewn with blood and nearly a dozen dead or dying men and woman. More than twenty zombies kneeled over the bodies scattered throughout the waiting room and pulled vital organs from their twitching hosts. It was nearly dark outside beyond the few windows within the waiting room. Flashing red and blue lights from police cars outside created a wave of endless colored lights along the interior walls. Alpert and a zombie in a white lab coat, painted red with blood, played tug-o-war with a man's intestines, attempting to take them from the other. They grunted and snarled for possession of the coveted, sausage-like meal. Men in biohazard suits walked past the main doors and looked inside. A few zombies looked up from their meal at the passing men, but they weren't interested in seeking out more dinner. Most returned to their current feast and ignored the men outside.

Rose approached the glass doors in less of a hurry while chewing on a severed forearm. The hand was still attached with a cell phone firmly clutched within it. The expensive cell phone chirped a musical tune as the face lit up. Rose stopped her approach to the door and the men in yellow plastic suits. She looked quizzically at the chirping cell phone, lifted it to her ear, and then reconsidered her actions.

She placed it in her mouth and bit into the phone, cracking the plastic face. She pulled the phone from her mouth and grunted, seemingly displeased with the taste. She tossed the arm aside and continued closer to the door and the man standing on the other side. She paused before the door and stared at the man in the plastic suit beyond it. He stared back at her in silent observation. She placed her bloodstained hand to the glass near him. He hesitated and placed his gloved hand to the glass on the other side. It seemed unusual that she'd actually retained some of her prior thoughts and emotions. She slowly reached for the bar to open the door, but it didn't budge. She tried again, but it still wouldn't open.

The man in the suit signaled to a soldier nearby. The soldier quickly approached with what appeared to be a dogcatcher's pole. The soldier readied himself while the man from CDC unlocked the door. Rose looked at the lock as it clicked. She looked back at both men and waited with an almost childlike innocence. The man from CDC opened the door only a couple of inches, allowing the soldier to slip the noose in through the opening. Rose watched the noose rise past her face, about to slip over her head. She suddenly grabbed the pole while snarling and yanked on it with all her might. The soldier was pulled forward and crashed into the partially open door, pinching his arm in the opening. He fought to pull his arm from the door and the pole free from her grip. He appeared ready to release the pole in order to free his arm.

"My arm is stuck!"

"Don't let her go," the man from CDC muffled a yell through his mask.

The solider struggled for control over the pole. Alpert was suddenly alongside Rose and grabbed onto the pole as well. He yanked on it, pulling the soldier's pinched arm further in through the opening. Rose grabbed his hand and bit his arm through his shirt. The soldier cried out in agony and struggled to pull his arm away from her teeth. Alpert attempted to grab the soldier's flailing arm before he could break free. The soldier pulled his arm free from Rose's grip and back outside before Alpert could grab it. Having seen the aftermath within the waiting room, Alpert almost certainly would have chewed his arm off. The soldier clutched his bleeding arm as the man from CDC locked the door.

Rose pressed her hands and face against the glass and watched both men, again with childlike innocence. She had managed to lure them in with a false sense of security. Had she lured them in on purpose? The man from CDC checked the soldier's bleeding arm. The solider looked up and was about to question his chances when the man from CDC pulled a semiautomatic from his holster and shot him in the head without hesitation. Blood and brains splattered against the glass near Rose's face. She watched as the soldier slid down the door to the sidewalk. She tilted her head with a curious look. Was her look sympathy or just hunger?

Chapter Twenty-four

*N*athan entered the morgue with a file in his hand and a perplexed look on his face. He shook his head as he approached Lexx, who stood over Ava's sheet covered corpse on the freezer slab. Hill attempted to look anywhere but at the corpse.

"I've never heard so many sirens before," Nathan announced. "Something big must be going on outside." He handed Lexx the file and eyed Ava's covered corpse. "You didn't honestly think someone slipped Dr. Kirby back into the morgue while I wasn't looking, did you?"

She ignored the question and drew a deep breath. "How would you feel about performing a tox screen on her?"

"It's within my power to conduct a tox screen," he replied then eyed Lexx suspiciously. Nathan appeared able to read her mind and gently tilted his head in question. "Is it just me, or is something bothering you, my dear?"

She fidgeted knowing he was sensitive to her moods, but she couldn't help the hostile feelings she harbored for him at that moment. "I'm having a bad day," Lexx replied gently without looking at him.

Nathan opened Ava's chart, glanced at Lexx, and then wrote an order on the physician's page. "Maybe it's just me, but I feel you have daggers in your eyes for me tonight. You're acting very strange."

Lexx shifted and held back her hostility. She wished she didn't like and respect him so much. "I'm sorry if you think I'm taking out my frustrations on you," she announced and forced a sigh. "I'm just a little cranky about misplacing a client. Carson's going to kill me when he finds out."

Nathan offered a sympathetic smile then removed several empty viles and a syringe. "To be honest," he announced, "I lost a corpse once myself."

Hill watched Nathan draw blood from the dead woman and grimaced. "This day officially sucks."

He walked across the room to get as far away from the corpse as possible. Hill removed his cell phone, attempted to place a call, and then frowned with disgust. Nathan eyed him and appeared humored by his ignorance.

"We're in a basement, remember?" Nathan announced with a hint of mockery in his tone. "Too much concrete. Use the in-house phone. Press nine for an outside line."

Hill remained disgusted as he approached the phone on the wall near the counter and pressed nine. He appeared bewildered and eyed Nathan, who busily worked on drawing blood from the chilled dead woman.

"I'm not getting an outside line."

"Did you press nine?" Nathan asked.

"I'm not stupid," Hill snapped. "I pressed nine. There's no outside connection."

Nathan set a vile on the counter and snatched the phone from him. "That's impossible. If there's an in-house connection, there has to be an outside one."

Nathan pressed an outside line, appeared dumbfounded, and then dialed the operator. Although the phone rang, there was no response. He pressed another number, and the phone in his office rang. He hung up and appeared baffled.

"No one's answering upstairs," Nathan remarked then sank into thought. "I wonder if that has something to do with the sirens outside." He looked at the smoke alarm. Nothing flashed. "If there had been a fire, the alarm would have sounded and the lights would be flashing."

Lexx approached, picked up the phone, and dialed a different number. The phone was answered and a woman's voice was heard on the other end.

"Hello?" the woman on the other end said into the phone. "Who is this?"

It was a strange response. Usually the nurses on the fourth floor answered the phone with 'ICU'.

"This is Lexx Davenport, I'm in the morgue with the coroner," Lexx announced and remained curious. "We can't get an outside line."

"Of course you can't," the woman scoffed lowly. "All communication with the outside has been cut off. We can't even use our cell phones."

Lexx's expression dropped. "What? Why?"

"Why?" the woman squawked. "Haven't you looked outside? CDC has the entire hospital locked down. Didn't you hear about the incident on the first floor?" The tone in the woman's voice was unprofessional, and it suddenly occurred to Lexx that this person probably wasn't even a hospital employee who'd answered the phone. "It's a war zone down there. It might be terrorists. No one's sure. Either way, no one is allowed in or out of the building. We were told to lock the fire doors on all floors. We aren't supposed to let anyone on or off our floors."

"No, we hadn't heard about that," Lexx announced and remained stunned. "Thank you for the update."

She hung up the phone and looked at both men, who now stared at her while waiting for a recap of the unusual conversation. She hesitated a moment as she attempted to make sense of what she had just heard.

"What is it?" Hill suddenly asked. "I don't like that look on your face."

"Someone at the ICU nurse's station said CDC locked down the hospital. No one is allowed in or out." She shook her head with disbelief. "All floors have been ordered to lock the fire doors. There was some sort of incident in the E.R."

"Wait, you mean we're trapped down here?" Hill suddenly demanded.

"No reason to panic, Sheriff," Nathan announced and seemed more calm then either Hill or Lexx. "The CDC likes to flex its muscles from time to time. In an hour or two, they'll realize it's nothing and everything will return to normal. If you work here long enough, you eventually see it all." He snorted a soft laugh. "And trust me, I've seen it all."

There was a commotion in the corridor, alerting all three. Hill hurried to the door and opened it with more vigor than he'd intended. Carson, Rolan, and Warren hurriedly rolled the casket along the corridor.

"What the hell--" Hill exploded.

"Carson?" Lexx gasped with surprise.

She couldn't believe her brother was in the basement and pushing a casket from their display room, one of the more expensive caskets at that. Carson and Rolan stopped and looked at Lexx standing in the doorway alongside Hill.

"Lexx, what are you doing here?" Carson suddenly asked while staring at his sister. The concern on his face seeing her within the hospital was frightening.

"It's a long story," she replied and again eyed the expensive casket. "What are you doing with that casket?"

"That's an even longer story," Carson muttered.

"Save it for family night," Warren growled. "We need to get this to the laboratory."

Carson and Rolan continued pushing the casket along the corridor on Warren's command. Lexx and Hill hurried after them. Nathan turned and looked back at the woman lying on the slab within the open freezer door. He approached the dead woman, took a deep breath, and leaned over her on the slab.

"You and I are in for a long night," he informed the dead woman.

He straightened and returned to the counter for the empty blood viles. Ava's eyes suddenly opened.

Chapter Twenty-five

At the opposite end of the basement corridor, Lexx and Hill followed the three men and the casket into the lab. Lexx was anxious to find out what was going on and why her brother and associate were being so secretive. Whatever happened had them rattled. A paper cut was usually enough to rattle Carson, but Rolan exercised nerves of steel. The blood on the lab floor had been hastily cleaned, leaving a pink stain, although no one seemed to notice. The sheet-covered body on the exam table with blood covering it was the main focus of their attention. If that wasn't enough to send minds reeling, what they saw in the corner definitely did the trick. In the corner, there was another blood-soaked sheet covering a small mass on the floor. As they looked from the covered corpse on the stretcher to the covered mass on the floor, the others shared the same concern for their situation.

Gunther sat at the counter and was so preoccupied with his work that he hadn't even looked up when they entered. He turned toward the casket then appeared surprised when he saw Sheriff Burke staring at the bloody mass in the corner of the room. The doctor immediately tensed then covered his emotions with a slight grin. He wasn't very convincing.

"Sheriff, how nice of you to join us in quarantine," Gunther announced almost pleasantly.

The sheriff wasn't in the mood to humor the chief surgeon. "Skip the pleasantries," Hill snapped and gave a nod to the mass in the corner and the body on the table. "What the hell is going on here?"

Gunther ignored the sheriff's question and glared at Warren. "Did you bring enough friends, Warren?"

"They'd already been exposed at the funeral home," Warren announced and gave him a secret signal with his raised brows. "I had *no* choice."

"Exposed?" Carson suddenly gasped and looked from Warren to Gunther. "What were we exposed to?"

Gunther ignored Carson's question and stared at Warren with surprise. "You mean she was infected?"

There was a dull thumping from within the casket. Lexx and Hill jumped back with surprise and stared at it. Neither could believe the sounds they were hearing. It sounded as if they had locked a live person inside the casket. Warren casually looked from the thumping casket to the doctor.

"Something like that," Warren replied with little emotion while placing his hands in his pockets.

The look on Hill's face was somewhere between alarm and panic. He looked from Warren to the doctor. "Someone had better start explaining fast," he lashed out, losing his patience.

Gunther finally looked at Hill and inhaled deeply while attempting to sound calm. "There's been an infectious outbreak in the E.R., and CDC has sealed the entire building," he explained. "The infection is contained on the main floor, but there's no telling how many have been exposed." He casually indicated the thumping casket. "The funeral home received an infected corpse, so I had Warren bring it back. If I can isolate the virus, I may be able to create an antidote."

"Whoa, wait a minute," Lexx announced while waving her hands around then indicated the expensive casket. "Are you telling me the person thumping around in that casket is a corpse?"

"It's true, Lexx," Rolan gently informed her and nodded to the casket. "It's Dr. Kirby."

"Dr. Kirby? She's alive?" Hill suddenly asked then became enraged. "Get her the hell out of there!" He appeared two seconds away from pulling his gun and shooting people.

"I wouldn't say she's exactly alive," Carson fumbled over his words.

"Well, she sure as hell can't be dead," Hill demanded and became more adamant. "Get her out of there!"

Gunther removed the sheet from Newman's body. There was a gunshot wound to his chest, and his shirt was soaked in blood. There was another gunshot to his forehead, but the small hole contained little to no blood.

"The infection drove Newman insane," Gunther announced. "When he attacked Frank, Warren was forced to shoot him." He indicated the gunshot wound to the chest. "Note the amount of blood from the wound." There was a moment of hesitation. "Obviously, Newman was killed from the initial gunshot to his chest. Moments after he died, he got back up."

Gunther then approached the mass in the corner and removed the sheet from what remained of Frank. He was eaten nearly beyond recognition, but his head remained intact. Lexx gasped and placed her hand to her mouth. Hill appeared sickened but was unable to look away.

"Our orderly there did this to the hematologist *after* he was dead." Gunther covered Frank's body. "That's where the second bullet wound came into play." He indicated the gunshot to Newman's forehead. "Note the minimal blood loss. He had already lost most of his blood before he'd been shot in the head." He approached the casket and casually leaned on it. "The infection is spread by saliva to blood contact. One bite and you're infected." He looked at Rolan and Carson and appeared curious. "Neither of you were bitten, I hope."

"Not for her lack of trying," Rolan muttered.

"And you're telling us what happened down here is what happened in the emergency room?" Hill asked with concern. He was actually starting to collect himself.

"Exactly," Gunther announced. "The only way to stop the infection is by stopping brain function. Anything else will only slow them down. I need Dr. Kirby alive, well, functioning. By examining her, I can maybe reverse what happened upstairs." He eyed the others in the room. "I'm going to need your help to do that. When this casket is opened, we need to immobilize her without destroying her brain."

"Not to sound like a smartass, but how do you propose we do that?" Rolan suddenly asked.

Gunther removed a broomstick with a chain fixed on the end in a loop. "Like a dogcatcher's pole."

He handed the homemade pole to Rolan, who frowned in response. "Thanks."

Gunther handed Hill and Warren each a crutch. "The two of you will hold her back while the inquisitive one slips the chain around her neck," Gunther informed them. "We can then safely tie her up, so I can do some experiments on her blood and tissue." He looked at Carson and raised a brow in question. "You're the funeral director, right? Can you unlock the casket?"

"I can, but I really don't want to."

Carson approached the casket and worked on the locking device. Tracy was heard thumping inside like a wild animal attempting to claw its way out. Once the casket was unlocked, Warren nodded to him. Carson pulled open the upper half of the lid and promptly hid behind it. The naked, dead woman sat up and grabbed for them. Hill appeared horrified while Warren attempted to keep her from standing by thrusting the broad end of the crutch against her. Hill was finally jolted into reality and helped hold her halfway in the casket with his own crutch. Rolan slipped the chain around her neck where she sat and kept her from standing. She clutched at the pole but couldn't free herself. As she attempted to grab them, Hill stared at the crudely missing fingers on her hand.

"What happened to her fingers?" Hill gasped with a sickened expression.

"She wasn't exactly cooperative," Rolan replied. "They sort of broke off when we closed the lid."

Hill looked as if he was about to throw up.

Chapter Twenty-six

There were no windows within the doctor's lounge on either the inside walls to the corridor or to the outside world. It seemed odd that an area where doctors went to get some well-deserved rest wouldn't have one of the nicer views of town or at the very least windows to provide sunlight. The clock on the wall informed the ten survivors sitting around the lounge that it was now dark outside. It seemed like days rather than hours. One of the survivors remained close to the thick door and attempted to listen to sounds coming from the emergency room corridor in hopes to hear something useful. He'd look at the group every so often and shake his head, indicating he'd heard sounds of the infected walking into walls and occasionally groaning.

Ellen clung to her mother's arm while resting her head on her shoulder, attempting to get some sleep. Pricilla patted her daughter's head and stared off at nothing in particular. One of the remaining live nurses tended to the bite on the woman's arm. The injury didn't seem that bad, despite the discolored discharge coming from the wound, but the woman appeared to be in severe discomfort. It didn't seem right that she should be in so much pain from such a small injury. The nurse was able to find painkillers in one of the doctor's lockers in the locker room. It was strange that they were there, but no one was questioning that right now. A thumping was heard from the doctor's shower room just beyond the locker room. No one reacted and none seemed interested in investigating the sound. Pricilla shifted uncomfortably, waking her sleeping daughter on her shoulder.

"Shouldn't we do something about that?" Pricilla finally asked the others.

Pricilla, Ellen, the nurse, and the injured woman were the only women holed up in the doctor's lounge. The other six were men. Two of the men shifted uncomfortably to her question. A third decided to get up and pace the length of the lounge, and the fourth remained positioned by the door, listening for anything useful. The remaining two men stood by the phone on the wall and talked with someone from another floor. Their conversations with others on floors above them were the only way to get information about what was going on. As the first man hung up the phone, the second man alongside him appeared interested.

"Well, what did they say?" he asked.

"Sit tight," the first man replied. "CDC is outside along with a dozen or more soldiers. Apparently, they're assessing the situation before making a plan."

"Sounds like bullshit," the nurse scoffed and checked on her patient, who now lie on the sofa.

The powerful pain medication was enough to put the injured woman to sleep. There was more thumping from beyond the locker room. Pricilla seemed to be the only one that heard it or possibly the only one who cared.

Pricilla grew impatient and became more demanding. "What are we going to do about that?" she asked firmly and made direct eye contact with Adam, the man near the phone, who had put himself in charge.

Adam wanted everyone to think he was tough, and perhaps he was tougher than those surrounding him at the moment, but he wasn't leader material.

"He's not going anywhere," Adam announced while standing straight, attempting to make himself look more authoritative. "As long as he's locked up in there, he's not a threat. If we open that door, we risk someone being ripped to shreds." He glared at Pricilla and raised his arrogant brows. "And you wouldn't want that, would you?"

Pricilla sneered her detest for the man and leaned closer to her daughter. "Reminds me of your step-father," she muttered. "Makes me glad he's gone."

Ellen sank back in her chair and frowned. "If we make it out of this in one piece, I'd like to take you up on your offer and move in with you."

Pricilla looked at her daughter with some surprise. "What changed your mind?" she asked then appeared curious to the conversation they hadn't had yet. "What *did* happen to that husband of yours?"

She appeared uncomfortable and shifted in her chair. "He ran out and left me there with one of those rabid people," Ellen remarked lowly. "That nurse from the front desk died saving me. But, you know what? I don't care about Peter. I just want to find Allison and get the two of you out of here. I'm not wasting any more energy worrying about that man."

She patted Ellen's arm reassuringly. "We'll find Allison," Pricilla announced. "She's resourceful. She can climb like a monkey and fit into really tiny places. I'm sure she found a place to hide."

Ellen took a deep breath and exhaled with a groan. She ran trembling fingers through her hair and avoided looking at her mother. "Maybe so, but she had a broken arm," she announced softly. "She certainly wouldn't be able to climb with a broken arm and in that dress." She started to sob and couldn't control her emotions. "She won't even be able to defend herself. Those things will tear her apart!"

Pricilla pulled Ellen's head to her chest and held her while she sobbed. By the look on her face, she was thinking the same thing but didn't want to admit it.

One of the men in the chairs across from them leaned closer to the second and muttered, "That's all we need--another hysterical woman."

Pricilla apparently heard the man and glared her annoyance. "Excuse me?" she demanded. "My granddaughter is out there somewhere. Her mother has every right to be upset." Her eyes narrowed to slits. "If there was a real man in this room, he'd be doing more than just sitting around."

The man was obviously offended and stood with hostility. "Hey, you should be grateful," he lashed out. "We're keeping your ass alive."

"How do you figure that?" Pricilla suddenly demanded in anger. She was about ready to jump out of her chair until Ellen grabbed her arm and held her back. "In what messed up world are *you* keeping *me* alive?"

"We're forced to remain here because of you women," he snapped. "We have your hysterical daughter, who's been sobbing since we got here." He indicated the sleeping woman on the sofa. "The woman who got a little scratch, acting like she was bitten by an alligator. And then you, the helpless, old woman complaining about everything. The only woman in this room of any real use is the nurse," he boldly announced.

All eyes were now on him. Even the men were stunned by the words coming out of his mouth.

"The rest of us would certainly be better off if we didn't have to look after the four of you," he remarked. "We'd be able to find a way out of here."

Pricilla was about to speak when Ellen pulled on her arm and threatened her with a look. It wasn't worth creating problems with others in such a confined space. Adam casually leaned against the wall and glared at the arrogant man standing in the middle of the room.

"That's enough out of you," Adam growled and appeared impatient. "Sit down and shut up, or you'll be the one we send out in search of help."

"You don't order me around," the man suddenly announced while glaring at Adam. "I don't know who the hell you think you are."

The injured woman lying on the sofa finally sat up and focused her attention on the man standing not far from her. He suddenly glared at her and appeared annoyed.

"Oh, the girl with the boo-boo wants to weigh in?" he snapped then snorted a laugh.

She kept her eyes locked on him without saying a word. He stared back, refusing to be intimidated by a woman he'd just ridiculed for being a crybaby. Her eyes were glossed over with that same dead look as those outside. His smile faded into concern as he stared at her. She suddenly snarled, leaped up from the sofa, and tackled him into the chair on the other side of the lounge. They crashed into the chairs, nearly taking out the second seated man. Both fell to the floor with the infected woman ending up on top. She tore into his throat as he screamed with pain and horror. Everyone within the room screamed as blood erupted from his jugular and sprayed across half the room.

Adam frantically searched around the waiting room for a weapon. He grabbed a chair and stood nearby while doing little more than watching the woman rip out the man's throat. Pricilla was immediately on her feet with the crutch in her hand. She swung for the woman's head as she tore flesh from the man's neck. The woman jerked from the head shot but didn't go down. She turned while straddling the man and snarled at Pricilla through bloodied teeth. Adam just stood and stared with horror, holding his chair. Pricilla cried out and struck the woman across the face with the crutch. She was thrown off the man and onto the floor. Several teeth flew from her mouth.

There was thumping against the lounge door followed by loud moans as the zombies attempted to get inside. The commotion stirred them, seemingly bringing them back to life. The zombie within the shower room was now thumping louder as well. Pricilla took a step back while clutching her crutch and stared at the motionless woman on the floor. Everyone finally breathed again. The woman suddenly scrambled to her feet, alarming everyone. Pricilla cried out and attempted to strike her again with the crutch, hitting her in the shoulder rather than the head. It barely slowed her down. The woman charged for Pricilla and knocked her onto the sofa. Pricilla attempted to push the snarling woman off her while keeping her teeth away from her face. Ellen grabbed the zombie by the arm and attempted to pull her off her mother. The zombie turned her head and snapped at Ellen's arm. Ellen screamed and released the arm.

Pricilla pushed the infected woman off her. She hit the floor, sprang to her feet, and lunged for Ellen. Adam leaped forward with the chair and plowed into the woman, driving her into the opposite wall with tremendous force. The metal leg of the chair penetrated her eye and plunged into her brain with a hideous crunching sound. She continued to thrash against the chair while Adam held her against the wall. Ellen joined him and gave an added thrust on the chair. There was another loud crunch. The zombie's thrashing finally subsided. Pricilla slowly stood with the help of her daughter. There was a thumping sound coming from above them. Everyone looked up, except Adam, who still didn't release the chair holding the dead woman to the wall. He was obviously in shock.

The thumping got louder above them. Pricilla allowed her eyes to fall across the room. The once annoying man was now on his feet with his throat torn out. Blood still flowed from his torn jugular and down the front of his shirt. He had the same dead look in his eyes. He snarled and charged for Pricilla and Ellen. Both women screamed. There was a loud crash from the ceiling as the vent flew open. The zombie turned to the sound. A black booted foot struck the man in the head with tremendous force. He immediately dropped to the floor. All eyes fell upon Monica as she straightened with a venomous look in her eyes. She was covered in dried blood and dirt from the vent.

Monica glared back at them. "Will someone tell me what the fuck is going on?"

Chapter Twenty-seven

*O*nly a few minutes had passed before Tracy was tied on the table that Newman once occupied. The naked dead woman struggled against the ropes, which bound her to the table. Gunther stood by her left side and removed several viles of blood while she snapped at him in an attempt to take a chunk from him. The others watched Gunther work while Hill paced the room. He was obviously upset that he was stranded in the basement while a riot of sorts was happening just one floor above him. It was his town, and he wanted to help control the situation. Once Gunther finished collecting blood and began analyzing it, Lexx lost interest and now watched Hill pacing the small lab. He was definitely the type of man who liked being physically active, which was probably why he chose police work.

Lexx preferred keeping her mind busy. She loved learning new things. She'd been involved in the embalming process since she was little. As a little girl, she'd watch her dad prepare a body and asked endless questions about tools he used and the purpose of each. It never occurred to her to be squeamish. While Hill was pacing the floor wishing he were upstairs; Lexx was dying to know how Tracy seemed to come back to life. She knew for a fact that the doctor had been dead.

"I need to access the situation upstairs," Hill finally announced and stopped pacing. "Is there a way up there?"

"Trust me, Sheriff, you do not want to go up there," Gunther informed him while remaining glued to his microscope. "When CDC finally goes in, they're going to shoot anything that moves. Anyone still breathing will have locked themselves somewhere safe by now. There's nothing you could do if you were up there."

Hill continued his pacing. The answer apparently didn't satisfy him.

Lexx watched him a moment longer. "You can go through the in-house phone directory and see if anyone answers," she announced. "We know floors two through six are secure, but there are dozens of phones on the first floor."

Hill eyed the struggling, naked zombie doctor and frowned. "I'll use the phone in the hall."

"I'd actually appreciate a quiet workspace, if you don't mind," Gunther announced and looked at the others within the lab. It was his polite way of telling them to leave.

Lexx, Hill, Carson, and Rolan willingly left the room. All four entered the hall and walked several feet away to the nearest hall phone.

Hill turned toward them and appeared defensive. "Is it just me, or does the chief surgeon seem to know a little more than he should?"

"And his right hand man is packing," Rolan informed them. "I saw his gun when we loaded the casket into the hearse. A little convenient he was armed when Newman *attacked* Frank."

"I'm a little skeptical of that orderly's death myself," Hill remarked, "but I have bigger concerns at the moment." He turned to Lexx. "You know your way around. What sort of weapons can we expect to find down here?"

She considered the question then mentally assessed the areas of the basement. "Well, we have physical and occupational therapy, the lab, morgue, and archives. There's the furnace room in the north end, maintenance just next to that, laundry, and storage."

"Rolan, Lexx, and I will check out maintenance and see what weapons we can create," Hill announced then turned to Carson. "I want you to stay with the coroner. Warn him about Dr. Sharp and his goon. I want you to keep an eye on him."

"Great. I get to pervert sit," Carson muttered.

"I'm certainly not leaving your sister alone with him," Hill remarked. "Watch for any signs of infected people down here and remember what the doctor said."

"Yeah, don't get bit or it's curtains baby," Carson said with a sigh.

Carson left the group and returned to the morgue just down the hall. He entered the morgue and suddenly hesitated. The door to freezer six was open, but the empty slab remained in the drawer. Nathan was conspicuously missing. Carson uncertainly looked around then became tense. He slowly approached the office with a concerned look.

"Dr. Oswald?" he said timidly while closely watching the office doorway.

Nathan appeared in the doorway, causing Carson to jump with surprise. Nathan took a sip of coffee from the mug he held and made a face.

"My coffee sucks," the coroner remarked lowly.

Nathan casually walked past Carson and shut the freezer door. As he turned, it again popped open. He groaned and slammed it shut. This time it remained shut.

"I wish maintenance would fix that," he remarked then glanced at Carson. "I ran tox screens on the corpses to see if I could determine what Dr. Sharp injected into their bodies." He casually leaned against the exam table. "There was an unknown drug in each of their systems but not the same unknown drug." He raised his brow with conviction. "I can't be positive, but I think our chief surgeon was experimenting on critical patients."

Carson appeared stunned. "Is that why Dr. Sharp thinks Tracy was infected with the same viral outbreak that turned the entire first floor into a blood bath?"

It was Nathan's turn to look surprised. He suddenly straightened. "There's a viral outbreak upstairs? What are their symptoms? Is that why the CDC is outside?"

"You didn't know?" Carson gasped while staring at him with surprise. "The infected people are *eating* the non-infected people. Dr. Sharp thinks it's transferred by blood and saliva. One bite and you're infected."

Nathan remained puzzled, set his coffee cup down on the exam table, and waved his hand. "Whoa, slow down. How does he know Dr. Kirby was infected?"

"Because she came back to life and tried to eat us," Carson interjected. "Who do you think was in that casket?"

"She came back to life?"

"Go look for yourself."

"She was at your funeral home," Nathan boldly announced. "How did he know her condition? Did you contact him with the information?"

"No, he sent Warren for Tracy's body," Carson announced. "He suspected she was infected--"

Nathan suddenly appeared deep in thought, causing Carson to immediately silence. Nathan stared at the floor a long moment then looked at Carson with his eyes wide as if suddenly putting everything together.

"He suspected she was infected, because he had prior knowledge," Nathan boldly announced. "If she saw something she shouldn't have, it could explain a lot."

"Are you suggesting Dr. Sharp threw Tracy down the stairs?" Carson suddenly gasped. His look turned hateful and moderately unpredictable. "That son-of-a-bitch!"

Nathan assumed a soothing tone in an attempt to calm his growing rage. "This is no time to go John Wayne, Carson. We're trapped in a pressure cooker with no way out."

Carson began to pace with a venomous look. There was no doubt he was entertaining different ways to end Gunther's life. He suddenly tensed, looked at Nathan, and appeared curious.

"Can it be spread through sexual contact?"

"During the incubation period?" Nathan questioned and uncertainly shook his head. "It would be like playing Russian roulette, but don't worry, Carson, she wasn't infected before the fall. When you and she would have--"

"I wasn't thinking about me," Carson suddenly snapped with a hostile glare at the coroner. He could barely control his anger toward Nathan any longer.

Gunther appeared puzzled while studying him. "There's something you're not saying." His look suddenly turned concerned as his eyes widened. "My God, is it Lexx?" he gasped. "Was she exposed while embalming Dr. Kirby and then had unprotected sex with someone?"

Carson stared at the coroner a long moment with his mouth hanging open. His anger quickly turned to shock. "My God, it wasn't you--"

"I'm sure it'd be worth risking infection," he announced simply, "but, I assure you, nothing happened between Lexx and I." He entertained a wayward thought and grinned. "Although I appreciate the vote of confidence." His look immediately turned serious. "Do you think she's been exposed? Is she showing any symptoms? Possibly flu like."

Carson couldn't tear his eyes away from Nathan. He finally broke the silence and spoke a little too quickly. "Uh, no. She's fine."

"Now you're not making any sense," Gunther remarked and impatiently folded his arms across his chest. His look was demanding. "Who had sexual contact with an infected person? It's important. They could be infected."

Carson fidgeted and subconsciously ran his fingers through his hair while fumbling with his words. "Someone violated Tracy's corpse."

There was an unbearable silence. Nathan suddenly cried out with horror, "Good God! That's--*disturbing*!" He suddenly fell silent and stared at Carson. The horror and disbelief showed on his face. "And you thought--?"

He suddenly fidgeted. "You were the last person with access to her body."

Nathan appeared almost too shocked to respond. When he finally did, he nearly exploded. "She was dead two hours before I got her," he announced firmly. "Her family wanted to pay their respects. She was only here ten minutes before Rolan came for her. I hadn't even popped her in the freezer yet." His look turned serious. "Whoever did that is at high risk of infection--*localized* infection."

Carson stared at him a moment as if not understanding. His eyes suddenly widened. "You mean--?"

Nathan nodded. "Yes, localized there."

Chapter Twenty-eight

The massive, cluttered maintenance shop was filled with broken beds, wheelchairs, stretchers, machinery, and various other objects in need of repairs. Rolan sharpened an old ax he'd found. On the table next to him, there was a spade shovel transformed into a large headed spear, a hacksaw blade welded onto the end of what used to be a rake, something homemade that now resembled a sling blade, and a wet saw blade welded onto an ice spade. Lexx brought a box to Hill, who sat at the counter and fiddled with what was once a leather tool belt. Lexx set the box on the counter near him and couldn't help grinning.

"Here are the tools you asked for, MacGyver," she announced teasingly.

Hill set down the belt and routed through the box of tools she'd brought. He seemed so serious in his work; it made her wonder if there was cause for alarm. She wished she knew what was going through his head.

"I hope you're doing all of this for nothing and not because you're anticipating a battle," Lexx said, suddenly realizing she had spoken aloud.

He briefly cast a glance at her and continued searching through the tools. "I'm doing this because I saw a very dead woman leap out of a casket intent on eating me," he remarked sternly. "I'm not exactly thrilled about being a Man-wich." He shook his head and muttered softly, "She's hated me since high school." Hill removed the leather tool belt, turned toward her, and appeared serious. "Hold your arms up."

Lexx gave him a bewildered look. She wanted to question the comment about Dr. Kirby, but decided against it and did as he asked. He placed the belt around her waist, measured visually, and then returned to the counter. He was a curious man.

"Should I ask?"

He either didn't hear her question or was simply ignoring her, which seemed more likely. "I saw a backpack near the office. Would you grab that?"

Lexx frowned and headed for the office. If he was going to order her about, he could at least let her in on his thought process. She grabbed the backpack with mild disgust and returned to him at the counter. He cast a quick look at the bag and returned to his work.

"Dump it out."

Lexx dumped the contents onto the counter and tossed the bag aside.

Hill looked at her and appeared bewildered. "I actually wanted the bag."

Lexx really wondered what he was up to now. She picked up the discarded bag and placed it on the counter before him. He turned back to her, placed the tool belt around her waist, and buckled it. She eyed the belt that now looked more like a holster. Without warning, he reached through her legs and adjusted a strap around her thigh. Lexx was startled by his initial actions then relaxed as she watched him attach the strap firmly around her thigh. Rolan approached with an armful of sharpened tools on sticks. He eyed Lexx as Hill placed various sharpened tools, including a hammer and screwdriver, within assigned slots inside the holster.

"Looking hot, Lexx," Rolan said with a grin.

As Rolan set down the tools, Hill tossed him a leather shoulder holster. Rolan eyed it, attempted to figure it out, and then slipped into it. Hill placed one of the long-handled tools resembling a sling blade through a slot in the back of his shoulder holster.

"Practice removing and replacing that until it feels comfortable," Hill instructed.

Rolan attempted to remove the makeshift sling blade from his back holster and nearly struck Hill in the head with the blade. Hill jumped with surprise and stared at Rolan with shock. He pointed across the room.

"Over there!"

Rolan smiled with embarrassment and hurried away. Hill shook his head and attempted to relax. Lexx watched as he cut the straps from the backpack and began working on a shoulder holster for himself. She couldn't deny his warrior mentality was a bit of a turn-on.

"You're scary prepared, Sheriff," she remarked while folding her arms across her chest. She stared at him longer than she should have. "And you call me creepy."

He continued to work without looking at her, remaining engrossed in creating his holster. "You know how kids make forts and play war?"

Lexx suddenly fidgeted. "Carson and I didn't really play those games."

They played other games as kids, but she couldn't tell him that she and Carson would pretend the caskets were racecars. Probably even worse was the time they played vampires in the casket room. Their games sometimes involved other children in the neighborhood, but usually only once. Oddly, the other children didn't like their games.

"Monica would set booby traps around her fort," he informed her. "She'd trapped me and three other boys in a pit for nearly two hours before my parents found us." He finally looked at her and frowned. "Growing up with 'little Miss Rambo' as your sister, you'd better learn to improvise. I'm sometimes surprised I survived my childhood."

Lexx hid her smile.

Hill caught her smile, didn't appear amused, and returned to his work. "It's not funny."

"It is, actually," she said and held back her giggle. "I can't imagine someone like you being bullied by a girl."

Hill stopped working, set his tools down, and looked at her. "Someone like me?"

"Yeah, you know; the big, tough manly sheriff type."

He stared at her a moment and appeared curious. "If I didn't know better, I'd swear that was a compliment."

"You don't think I'm capable of compliments?"

"Not toward us regular people."

"Regular people?" she scoffed and felt the color rush to her cheeks. Her irritation surfaced, and she again found him insufferable. "You certainly come up with new and ingenious ways to insult me, don't you?"

"How is that an insult?" he suddenly remarked. "I'm the hick, country cop who threw up in your prep room. I doubt you think much of us average guys."

Lexx stared at him a moment with a look of surprise. It then dawned on her. Could it be true?

"You think I'm above you?" she suddenly asked.

"It's pretty obvious you are." He then muttered, "You studied to be a doctor, for Christ's sake."

Lexx sat on the table near him and offered a humored smile. Her insecurities toward him were quickly fading away. "That's kind of ironic; because I was pretty sure you were the one looking down on me."

"Why? Because I think you're creepy?"

"That might have something to do with it," she replied and shifted slightly. "Your squeamish nature toward my profession doesn't mean I think any less of you." She stared at the handsome sheriff possibly longer than she should have. "Professionally, I think you're both intimidating and impressive, and I'm sorry if I made you think I don't respect you."

Hill studied her a moment where she sat on the counter near him, leaned back in his chair, and suddenly grinned. "Are you hitting on me?"

Lexx felt her cheeks immediately redden to his comment. She didn't even know how to respond. He'd caught her completely off guard. She quickly stood and avoided looking at him, hoping he didn't see her reddened cheeks.

"What? No," she announced in a high-pitched squeal. She immediately cursed herself for the pitch of her voice and shifted with discomfort. "I hardly think this is the proper time and place for that sort of thing."

Hill stood directly in front of her and prevented her from moving away from the counter. She was forced to meet his gaze and oddly serious look.

"I disagree," he replied. "I'm not exactly thrilled with our situation and even less happy to speculate about what's going on upstairs."

There was an odd silence. She couldn't look away from his ice blue eyes.

"I haven't been on a date in months and celibate longer than I'm willing to admit," he remarked and moved closer to her, now leaving less than an inch between their bodies. "I wouldn't mind an attractive woman hitting on me just once before I do something stupid and get myself killed."

Lexx stared at him with a strange look as many thoughts shot through her head. With everything he admitted and the sexual desire rushing through her, there was only one thing she could think to say in response.

"You're not thinking about going upstairs, are you?" she suddenly demanded.

He frowned and took a step away from her. It was hard to tell if he was disappointed that she didn't take the bait or lost enthusiasm after her sobering comment.

"I'm the sheriff," he informed her. "I'm supposed to look after the people of this town. We don't know what's going on up there. We don't know that it's a total loss. They may need my help." His look turned serious and almost fearful. "Monica was working tonight," he said gently. "The ambulance was parked outside when we pulled up. What if she's up there?"

She knew how he felt. She'd feel the same way if Carson's fate was uncertain, although, Carson was less able to take care of himself. Monica could certainly handle herself.

"I know you're worried about her, but you can't go up there," she insisted. "You heard what Dr. Sharp said. It's a battlefield up there."

"I know what he said, but I need to see for myself," he announced. "I can't just sit here and do nothing."

Lexx drew a deep breath and stared at him. That's why he wanted to make weapons. He wanted to go upstairs. He had every intention of going up there. Hill stared back with a lost look in his blue eyes. She knew she shouldn't say it, but she couldn't help herself.

"I've been running around this hospital since I was a little girl," she informed him. "If I tell you how to get upstairs unseen and unnoticed, do you promise to only make a quick observation and not do anything stupid?"

Hill appeared surprised and studied her. He seemed ready to jump out of his skin. "You know a way upstairs that won't be blocked?"

"I'm relatively confident it hasn't been sealed."

"If you show me a way upstairs, I'll promise anything you want."

She didn't trust him. He was going to do something stupid, and she never should have told him she knew a way upstairs. Lexx had to think of a way to make him keep that promise.

"Then you won't have a problem with me going along," she announced.

He stared at her and seemed to stop breathing. "I'd rather you didn't. It's too dangerous."

"It shouldn't be, not if you're just making a quick observation," she replied with a cocky tilt of her head. "I'll remind you that you're also responsible for my safety. That should keep you from doing something stupid."

He stared at her a long moment then frowned. "Remind me not to play poker with you."

Chapter Twenty-nine

*R*olan and Hill followed Lexx across the massive laundry room filled with racks of linens, folding presses, tables, and large bins of dirty laundry. They headed toward the small dumbwaiter beyond large, industrial sized washing machines and dryers. Rolan casually leaned against a rack containing scrub uniforms. Hill looked at the small metal door with surprise then looked back at Lexx and shook his head.

"I don't think I'll fit in there."

"The dumbwaiter hasn't worked in years," she informed him then opened the small door. There was an opening to the shaft with rungs up the back wall. "The rungs go all the way to the sixth floor with access to the linen closets on each floor."

Hill stared up the shaft then looked back at Lexx. The look of concern on his face showed. "It's too narrow," he announced. "I can't let you come along."

She glared her disapproval. "Oh, no, you don't."

"If I have to climb down in a hurry, you'll be in my way," he informed her.

Lexx folded her arms across her chest and glared at him with an annoyed look. "Fine, then I'll just continue up to ICU on the fourth floor and check on Brandon."

He was becoming quickly annoyed with her attitude. "You're not going up that shaft."

"And just how do you intend to stop me?"

Rolan hid his smirk and appeared to be enjoying the exchange. Apparently, he'd lost many arguments with Lexx in the past. Hill stared at Lexx a moment then looked at Rolan, who watched the exchange.

"Can you talk some sense into her?" Hill asked.

Rolan appeared surprised. "Who? Me?" he squawked then shook his head. "Are you kidding? She's my boss. Besides, she'll kick my ass. She's not a sweet as she looks."

Hill looked back at Lexx. She smirked knowing she'd won that round. She attempted to crawl through the opening. Hill stopped her and pointed a warning finger at her.

"You stay behind me," he threatened, "and you do exactly what I tell you. Got it?"

She nodded her response. Hill took a deep breath and climbed through the opening beyond the sliding door. He climbed several rungs before Lexx climbed into the elevator shaft behind him. She followed him up the rungs in the narrow shaft. He moved slower than she had anticipated. Apparently, he was apprehensive about the climb, but she had done it many times as a child. When the dumbwaiter had broken for the final time, the hospital went to the easier linen cart system. Orderlies tended to overstuff the dumbwaiter with linen, creating a difficult job for the laundry staff. They finally reached the dumbwaiter door on the first floor. Lexx waited while Hill slid open the door and inspected the linen closet before climbing out.

Lexx was about to climb out after him when he held up his hand, stopping her. He hurried to the linen closet door, locked it, and then motioned for her to join him. Lexx climbed through the opening and looked around the linen closet. It was undisturbed. There were no sounds beyond the closet, which surprised both. Considering Gunther's take on what was happening on the first floor, they expected a lot of commotion and mass hysteria. She wondered why it was so quiet beyond the door. Both positioned themselves alongside the door. Hill removed his ax while Lexx removed a hammer from her holster. He silently unlocked the door and gently pulled it open just enough to peer into the corridor. He appeared bewildered and slowly opened the door. Hill and Lexx stood in the doorway and looked up and down the empty emergency room corridor. There was blood everywhere but not a single person, dead, alive, or any state in-between. Both appeared bewildered and entered the hallway. Neither moved away from the safety of their linen closet.

"Do you think CDC came through already?" Lexx asked softly more to herself.

He slowly shook his head while remaining alert. "We would have heard shots," Hill informed her. "You stay here. I'm going to have a look around."

Hill quietly walked down the hall. Lexx quietly closed the linen closet door and followed after him. He glared at her, but she ignored his look. The amount of blood was staggering. Lexx couldn't even recall a scene from any horror movie that came close to what she was witnessing. There was stray body parts scattered around the once white corridor, which was alarming in itself. Judging by the way Hill eyed each gnawed limb, he wasn't holding up nearly as well as he'd have her believe. Despite things Lexx had witnessed in her years as a mortician, this was the most disturbing thing she'd ever seen. The fate of those occupying the hallway at the time frightened her more than she cared to admit. As they passed a nearly intact man sprawled along the floor, Lexx found herself staring helplessly at what had once been a janitor. He appeared to be missing an arm and most of his face as he lie face down in his own blood. She couldn't help but wonder why his was the only intact body within the corridor. More importantly, where were the rest of the bodies? They approached the doors to the waiting room. The absence of sound chilled her more than the gruesome images remaining in the blood.

A strange thumping sound was heard above them, startling both. They suddenly hesitated and looked at the ceiling. Obviously, there was nothing there. They looked back to the lobby doors. A blood covered zombie nurse resembling Patty, with her head resting on her shoulder, stood before the door holding a severed arm in her hands. She chewed on the arm while staring at them then snarled.

"I have an idea," Lexx said softly. "Let's go back to the linen closet."

"It's just one," Hill announced while clutching his ax. "We can take her."

The double doors to the emergency waiting room opened to reveal two dead men covered in blood. Behind them, the lobby was filled with mutilated undead men and women meandering about with little purpose.

"I'm going to listen to you more," Hill muttered in a soft tone. "Nice and easy--back to the linen closet."

Both slowly turned in hopes that lack of sudden movements would attract less attention. Several zombies approached from the opposite end of the hall, blocking their path to the linen closet. For a brief second, no one dead or alive moved.

"I wish I'd stayed in the basement," Lexx muttered and attempted to open the door near them. It was locked!

Hill readied his ax then looked at the dead janitor lying on the floor just a few feet away. Hill's eyes lit up.

"Keys," he cried out softly.

Lexx saw the keys attached to the janitor's pants. She slid onto the floor near the dead man, avoiding the blood, and attempted to remove the ring as the zombies watched them from both ends. She pulled the keys free and smiled with relief. The janitor's eyes suddenly opened, and he grabbed for her. Lexx screamed and sprang to her feet. Hill stepped forward, swung the ax, and struck the janitor in the back. It stopped him momentarily, but he again attempted to get up. Hill pulled his ax free to the sound of crunching vertebrae and jumped back with surprise. Lexx tried keys in the lock with trembling hands. Hill moved closer to her and watched the janitor slowly move to his feet.

"Can you work a little faster?"

"I'm trying," she snapped softly.

The zombies from both ends snarled and charged them. The lock on the door sprang open. Hill pushed Lexx into the room and slammed the door behind them. The zombies crowded the door and pawed at it, attempting to get inside. Hill locked the x-ray waiting room door while a horde of zombies thumped against it from the other end. Lexx nervously looked around the waiting room then to the open door leading into another corridor. Lexx nudged Hill. He approached the corridor with his ax. Lexx followed behind, leaving little space between them. A zombie suddenly struck the glass window to the nurse's office. Both jumped back with surprise and stared at Peter with half his face chewed off. The zombie x-ray technician soon joined him by the window.

Hill indicated the door beyond the zombies. "The door is closed," he announced. "They're trapped inside for the moment. We'll rig it shut to be safe." He motioned for her to follow him toward the nearby corridor.

Lexx and Hill walked along the narrow corridor with their weapons raised and looked at the nurse's office door. It was already crudely barricaded. They exchanged bewildered looks and continued onward to the bathroom and changing room. Nothing moved and everything seemed quiet. Of course, so had the emergency room. They approached the x-ray room near the back. A zombie in a scrub uniform leaped from the doorway for Lexx. Hill swung the ax, nicked the zombie's arm, and struck the wall. The zombie tackled Lexx to the floor as she screamed. Hill left the ax embedded in the wall and drew his weapon. Before he could even react, Lexx flipped the zombie off her and sprang to her feet. The zombie got up slower than Lexx. Hill shot the zombie in the leg, but it didn't even affect him as he continued to his feet.

"What's wrong with you?" Lexx cried out. "Head!"

Hill aimed with more determination and shot the zombie in the forehead. Its head snapped back as its skull exploded thick, dark blood and brains out the back. They watched the zombie fall to the floor. It no longer moved.

"Sorry. Shooting a suspect in the leg was drilled into me," he announced while trembling then looked her over quickly with concern. "He didn't bite you, did he?"

"No, but my back has felt better."

Hill looked into the MRI room and suddenly grimaced. The room was painted with blood and what remained of a nurse was scattered around haphazard. Her severed leg in a cast sent chills down Lexx's spine.

"What's left of that nurse can't hurt us," he informed her and appeared sickened.

"I'd better call Rolan and tell him we're going to be here a while," Lexx muttered.

"Now might be a good time to check with the other floors and see what they know," Hill informed her with a defeated sigh. He searched her eyes and appeared apologetic. "I'm sorry I got us trapped."

She managed a tiny smile. "Hey, we're still alive. That's all that matters."

Lexx heard the sound of something dull scraping metal. She hesitated and looked into the nearby room. The only thing in the room was the closed MRI machine, which resembled a doughnut with a long, hard table sticking out of it. She slowly entered the room and looked around. Hill entered behind her and kept watch behind them as well. Something scraped again. It came from the machine itself. Lexx slowly approached the machine with her hammer clutched firmly in her hand. Hill maintained some distance and looked around. The sound was heard again, and it was close, possibly coming from inside the machine. Lexx slowly moved around the machine to look behind it. A bare foot suddenly slid down the side of machine in front of Lexx's face. She cried out and jumped back with her hammer prepared to strike. Hill aimed his gun then hesitated. Ten-year-old Allison in her torn dress clung to the top of the machine with her one good arm and stared down at them. She looked terrified and attempted to pull up her bare foot as it scratched against the side of the machine.

"Hey," Lexx said softly while staring at her and returned her hammer to her holster. "It's okay. No one's going to hurt you. We won't hurt you."

"How do I know?" Allison gasped in a trembling voice.

"We're not infected," Lexx replied and attempted to sound comforting. She wasn't used to dealing with children, especially frightened ones. "It's okay. You can come down. No more can get in."

Allison didn't appear completely convinced, but since she was losing her footing and her grip, she reluctantly slid down the side of the machine. Lexx helped catch her at the bottom. The young girl had removed her shoes in order to climb the machine, and with only one good arm, that was amazing in itself.

"A man bit Marco. He bit him real hard that he bled," she said softly. "He told me to hide. Is he dead? Marco?"

"I'm not sure," Lexx said gently. "I don't know Marco."

"He has white hair and tattoos on his arms."

Hill suddenly grimaced. Lexx saw his look and didn't know what to say. She looked at the little girl's left arm and sat on the MRI bed to inspect it without lifting it.

"You've been injured," Lexx announced, attempting to change the subject.

"I fell from a tree," Allison said. "Marco said it was broken. Clean he said. He let me see the pictures. It hurts when I try to use it."

Lexx stared at the little girl then smiled gently. "Well, then, we should probably put that in a cast for you."

Hill looked away from the open door and stared at Lexx. "Do you know how to do that?"

"Premed, Sheriff," she casually replied. "I know a little about a lot. Since we're stuck here anyway, I may as well make her a little more comfortable."

Chapter Thirty

*G*unther sat at the counter testing blood samples while Tracy struggled against the ropes binding her to the table. Warren sat in a chair near the door and watched her in silence while he fiddled with his gun. It was uncertain whether he was intrigued by the dead woman mimicking life; or if he was waiting for an excuse to put a bullet in the beautiful zombie's head. Gunther appeared frustrated, shifted in his chair with a groan, and gingerly rubbed his infected arm. The dark, bloody substance continued to ooze through his lab coat sleeve. He gently rolled up his sleeve, looked at the oozing discharge saturating the gauze wrap, and appeared concerned by the coloring. He pulled a small case from his jacket pocket and removed a syringe and a small bottle. While Warren was preoccupied fiddling with his gun, Gunther drew solution into the needle and injected it into his arm near the wrapped injury. He cringed slightly then secretly returned the items to his lab coat. He took a deep breath and looked back into the microscope. After only a few seconds of staring at the slide on the glass, he appeared disgusted and turned away from the desk.

"I can't isolate the infection," he announced and looked at Warren. "I know what vile she'd been exposed to, but it didn't have these side effects on other test subjects." He shook his head while searching for an answer. "The nurse, EMT, Newman, and Dr. Kirby inhaled the gas, which eventually entered their bloodstream, mutated, and affected their tissue and organs. Because Dr. Kirby died before the infection took hold, it took longer to regenerate and bring her back." He leaned back in his chair. "I'm positive the antibiotics she was given right after she was infected slowed the progression as well. Beyond that, I have nothing."

"Are you any closer to finding a cure? Are you sure antibiotics won't cure the infection?" Warren asked and replaced his gun to his shoulder holster.

"No, even in high, concentrated amounts, they only slow its progression," he announced while subconsciously rubbing his wrapped arm then drew a deep breath. He pulled his lab coat sleeve over the edge of the wrapping to prevent Warren from seeing his injury. "I need an uninfected test subject."

Warren raised a curious brow and showed little emotion. "Blood sample or guinea pig?"

"Living tissue."

"Well, you're in luck, Doc," Warren informed him and offered an unsettling grin. "We have five guinea pigs chilling in the morgue down the hall."

"The sheriff may prove less than cooperative."

"You don't need to worry about him," Warren announced. "I can be very persuasive."

Gunther seemed unconvinced and gave him a stern look. "Remember I need them alive. They're no good to me if they're dead."

"How about slightly chilled?" Warren asked teasingly with a sly grin.

"Slightly chilled works."

Warren stood and casually left the lab. Gunther returned his attention to his microscope. Tracy snarled and thumped against her restraints, distracting him. Gunther looked back at her and stared at the thrashing, snarling dead woman. He drew a deep breath and leaned back in his chair.

"You know, Dr. Kirby," he announced gently, "it was nothing personal."

She snarled in response and kept her eyes locked on him. He fidgeted slightly. It was almost as if she was condemning him with her snarl. Gunther stood and approached the exam table to which she was bound.

"Maybe Newman took things a bit far by, you know, tossing you down the stairs." Gunther took a deep breath and leaned on the table, partially hovering over her. "But you had been warned to mind your own business. I mean, I'm chief surgeon of this hospital. You shouldn't have been poking around in my business like that in the first place." He hesitated while staring at her and again looked remorseful. "I never meant for any of this to happen to you." He frowned, shook his head, and gently brushed the hair from her face. "You were such a beautiful woman."

She again snarled and snapped at his hand touching her hair. He pulled his hand back with surprise, having nearly lost a finger to her teeth. As he stared at her, his expression turned less sympathetic and more cruel.

"Then again, perhaps you deserved everything you got," he remarked lowly.

Chapter Thirty-one

*W*arren headed down the excessively quiet corridor. It was hard to imagine the hell-raising scene upstairs and the mass chaos outside with how quiet things were underground. Warren entered the morgue and casually looked around. Carson and Nathan stood over the sterile exam table while playing a board game containing three game pieces. Rolan was stretched out on one of the freezer slabs with his eyes closed and his hands clasped behind his head near the opening. Carson and Nathan looked at Warren as he entered and appeared interested. Rolan quickly sat up on the slab and stared as well.

Warren looked around with a puzzled look. "What happened to the sheriff and that girl?" he asked.

"They're playing 'hide and seek'," Rolan teased with a lusty smile.

Carson frowned his disapproval.

"Dr. Sharp needs some help with one of his experiments," Warren informed them.

All three exchanged looks with great interest.

"If it brings him closer to a cure--" Carson announced, seemingly volunteering.

"Exactly," Warren replied, removed his gun, and aimed it at them.

All three appeared alarmed and stood immobile while staring at the gun.

"What's with the gun, Warren?" Carson suddenly asked in louder tone than necessary.

Warren turned to Rolan on the slab without responding to Carson's question. "You stay where you are," he announced then looked at Nathan. He waved his gun, indicating Rolan. "Push him in the freezer."

Nathan appeared alarmed as his mouth fell open. "That'll kill him."

"So make sure you turn the temperature up to a healthy level," Warren announced simply then turned impatient. "Let's go. We haven't got all day."

Nathan uncertainly approached Rolan, who appeared concerned while lying back on the metal slab. Nathan pushed the slab with Rolan on it into freezer six, gave him a reassuring look, and shut the door.

"Now you, doc," Warren announced.

Nathan adjusted the freezer control and opened the freezer door below Rolan's freezer. He uncertainly moved onto the slab while glaring at Warren and his gun.

Warren motioned to Carson. "Push him in."

Carson reluctantly pushed the slab containing Nathan into the freezer and shut the door. He stared at the freezer door containing Rolan only a moment, held his breath, and then looked back at Warren.

"Now you and I are going to join Dr. Sharp and your girlfriend."

Carson skeptically walked to the morgue door with Warren following. The phone receiver was missing from the base on the nearby wall. The receiver lie on the desk with the red speaker light glowing.

†

*A*t the same time, just upstairs in the x-ray department, Lexx stood by the phone in the waiting room. The red speaker light was lit on the phone alongside her. She disconnected the call and turned to Hill with a look of alarm on her face. Hill was already pacing the waiting room and didn't bother looking at Lexx. Allison, who had been drawing on her pink cast with a permanent marker, stopped and looked at them as well.

"Dr. Sharp is going to do something to Carson," she gasped. "We have to help him!"

"I know, I know," Hill announced and appeared to sink into thought. He checked the clip in his gun and frowned. "I have four rounds and an extra clip. There's no telling how many of them are out there."

"We have the weapons."

"And they have sheer numbers," he reminded her. "If they mob us, we're done. I can't risk the little girl." He hesitated, drew a deep breath, and stared at Lexx a moment. "You stay here with Allison. I'll get Carson back."

"Sheriff--" she protested.

There was a strange thumping from the ceiling. It was the same sound they'd heard in the corridor. Hill aimed his gun at the ceiling while Lexx forced Allison behind her and grabbed the ax. All three stared at the ceiling and listened to the sound. The sound appeared to be traveling the length of the ceiling.

"There's that sound from the hallway," Lexx gasped softly while clinging to the ax.

The ceiling grate suddenly swung open, alarming both. They raised their weapons defensively toward the ceiling. Monica poked her head through the opening, saw them, and grinned. She possibly meant to startle them with her entrance.

"I've been looking all over for you guys," she announced almost cheerfully. "I was starting to think you didn't get away from those freaks."

Monica swung her legs through the opening and dropped to the floor below. As she dropped, Hill helped catch her. She took a quick step back from him, brushed some cobwebs from her bloodstained clothes, and eyed Lexx. She raised her brows sharply in question.

"I didn't interrupt anything between you and Snow White, did I?"

Lexx rolled her eyes. The woman was insufferable. It was possible the zombies didn't attack her, because they secretly feared her. Allison peeked out from behind Lexx and appeared distrusting of the aggressive woman.

Hill smiled with relief and hugged Monica. "I thought you were dead."

Monica pushed him away and glared at him. "Keep that sappy stuff to yourself," she snorted. "Of course I'm alive." She hesitated then sneered with disgust. "I'm not exactly thrilled about having to kill Evan to stay that way, but shit happens."

Hill appeared horrified while sweeping a look over her. She had a large amount of dried blood on her clothing. "He didn't bite you, did he?"

"Not for lack of trying," she replied. "I saw firsthand what happens to your ass if you're bit." Monica saw Allison peeking out from behind Lexx. She immediately tilted her head then eyed Hill. "How long was I gone?" Monica looked back at the little girl and smiled. "Hey, I remember you. You were in the emergency waiting room. Have you been hiding in here the whole time?"

Allison again hid behind Lexx and avoided Monica.

"Huh, I don't get it," Monica said. "Kids usually love me."

Hill looked at his sister, gently cleared his throat, and indicated the large amount of dried blood covering her uniform. "Your appearance may have something to do with that."

Allison again peeked out from behind Lexx and uncertainly pointed at her EMT badge. "Is that someone's finger?"

Monica glanced at her uniform, saw the partial finger caught behind her badge, and casually flicked it off her uniform. "Yeah, but I'm an EMT, we reattach those all the time."

The little girl still didn't know what to make of Monica. Lexx was happy Monica was making friends with the little girl, but she'd had enough of the small talk. Carson was in some sort of trouble, and they needed to act quickly before Dr. Sharp did something unthinkable to him.

"Is there a vent opening in the linen closet on this floor?" Lexx abruptly asked.

Monica eyed Lexx with bewilderment and raised a cocky brow. "I would assume so, but there's nothing we need there." She returned her gaze to her brother. "The others are in the doctor's lounge. We have enough coffee and snacks to hold us over until CDC grows a pair and gets in here."

"Others?" Hill asked with surprise. "How many others? Any of them bit?"

"Do you think I'm stupid?" she snarled while glaring at him. Monica collected herself and attempted to sound less hostile. "No, none were bit. We dealt with them."

"Dealt with them?" Hill suddenly asked.

"Yes, *dealt with them*," Monica hissed with a demanding look then indicated the frightened little girl. "Considering how daisy fresh you're looking, I'm guessing you've been sitting around twiddling your thumbs. There are eight survivors in the doctor's lounge." Monica looked at the little girl and again smiled. "Your mother will be happy to see you."

The little girl's face lit up. "My mother's there?"

Monica nodded. "She showed me your picture right before I climbed into the vent. Asked me to keep an eye out for you on my travels." Her look turned serious. "Follow me and keep quiet. I'll get you to the doctor's lounge."

Monica turned toward the vent and was prepared to jump for the edge when Hill stopped her.

"We have to get to the linen closet down the hall," Hill quickly announced. "Do you know the way to it?"

She suddenly turned and stared at both with annoyance. "Yeah, it's just beyond the doctor's lounge. What's with the linen closet?" Monica scoffed and eyed them demandingly. "You two have a hot date?"

Lexx was quickly losing patience with the insufferable woman and desperately wanted to lash out. "Dr. Sharp locked my assistant and the coroner in the morgue freezers," she boldly announced. "He took my brother at gunpoint and intends to do some sort of experiment on him."

"Experiment?" Monica suddenly gasped.

"We'll explain on the way," Lexx informed her unable to contain her anxiety. "There's a dumbwaiter shaft in the closet that'll take us to the basement."

"Dr. Sharp's goon is going to kill them if we don't get down there," Hill informed his sister. "You can take Allison to her mother, and we'll continue on to the linen closet."

Monica cocked her head and cleverly raised her brows. "And let you have all the fun? I don't think so. Let's go."

Monica looked at Allison and indicated the vent above her. She extended her hand to her. Allison took Monica's hand and allowed her to boost her up to the vent. Allison grabbed on to the edge and managed to climb in despite her pink cast.

"Wait for us," Monica informed the little girl in the vent opening. She eyed her brother and Lexx. "Oh, I'm sorry. Where are my manners?" Monica pulled a chair from the wall, placed it under the vent opening, playfully slapped it, and grinned at both while indicating the chair. "After you."

Hill rolled his eyes then looked at Lexx. "You'll have to forgive Monica," he announced. "We're thinking about having her balls snipped."

Lexx hid her smile. She enjoyed Hill's brazen comment a little too much. Monica just glared at Hill. He was going to pay dearly for that remark.

"At least one of us has balls," Monica retorted lowly so the little girl couldn't hear them. She glared at Lexx and indicated the vent. "You're next, princess."

Lexx sneered in response and climbed on the chair beneath the vent. Hill attempted to assist her. With some irritation, she motioned him to back off. He frowned and took a step back. Lexx swiftly pulled herself partway into the vent, allowing her legs to dangle a moment. She kicked out with her legs for added momentum, purposely kicking Monica in the face. Monica yelped and jumped back while clutching her cheek. She glared at the vent opening as Lexx's feet disappeared into the ceiling. Lexx turned within the vent, looked down at the stunned woman, and smirked deviously.

"I'm so sorry," Lexx hissed with bitterness. "I didn't see you there."

Monica sneered at Lexx while gently rubbing her red cheek. "You kick like a girl."

Lexx smiled and disappeared into the vent. Hill avoided looking at Monica so she wouldn't see the smirk on his face. Monica stopped him from climbing onto the chair. He looked back at her, groaned lowly, and folded his arms across his chest.

She indicated the opening in the vent. "You could do worse," Monica casually remarked.

Hill stared at her with surprise. She offered a tiny smile. Hill hid his smile and climbed on the chair.

Chapter Thirty-two

*W*arren forced Carson at gunpoint along the corridor in the direction of the lab. Both paused before the door and were about to enter when they saw Gunther slowly approaching from the opposite end of the hall. He had a look of horror on his face and appeared unable to speak. Warren stared at him with a puzzled look as he approached.

"Is something wrong, Doc?" Warren asked.

"I--I was just in the bathroom," Gunther fumbled and could barely get the words out.

Both watched him as he got closer with shared looks of concern. His color was off, although he wasn't showing symptoms as the others had.

"He doesn't look right," Carson muttered to Warren and attempted to take a step behind the man with the gun.

Warren grabbed Carson's arm and forced him to stand his ground. He clutched his gun while watching Gunther. "You feeling okay, Doc?"

"I'm, uh, fine," he said softly and held his head with a trembling hand.

As he got closer, they could see blood on his hand and discolored blood seeping through the crotch of his pants. Carson's eyes widened with horror and then turned to rage.

"It was you!" Carson exploded.

Warren appeared tense and uncertainly aimed his gun at Gunther. He cast a quick glance at Carson with a demanding look in his eyes. "What are you talking about?"

Gunther stopped his approach, realizing the gun was aimed at him, and then looked at the blood on his trembling hand. He looked back at Carson and Warren.

"I didn't do anything," Gunther insisted with less confidence and a look of fear on his face.

"He's been infected," Carson lashed out.

Warren appeared alarmed and aimed the gun at Gunther with more conviction.

"No, I haven't," Gunther gasped with the sound of fear in his voice. "Don't listen to him. You work for me, Warren, remember?"

"He molested Tracy's corpse," Carson cried out in rage while pointing wildly. "Nathan said it would cause infection at the contact site." He indicated the blood spreading across Gunther's crotch. "That's the contact site."

Warren appeared stunned then enraged, showing emotion for the first time. "You sick fuck!"

He was about to squeeze the trigger when the lab door opened to reveal the naked, dead doctor. Carson saw her and cried out with surprise. Warren spun with his gun aimed but wasn't fast enough. Tracy leaped onto Warren and bit him on the side of the neck. He cried out with surprise and ripped her off him before she could tear through his flesh. He shot wildly without aiming and hit her in the shoulder near her neck. She was jolted but continued for him. Warren pulled the trigger, but the gun clicked empty. Carson grabbed Warren and pulled him away before she could grab him. Carson hurried Warren down the corridor and away from Gunther and the dead woman. They ran inside the physical therapy department and slammed the door behind them. Tracy set her sights on Gunther as blood ran down her chin. He stared back at her with horror in his eyes. He backed away but appeared weak and uncoordinated. Despite her bone protruding out her lower leg, Tracy lunged for Gunther and tackled him to the floor, landing on top of him. Gunther attempted to hold her back while she straddled him and tried to bite his neck.

"No, Dr. Kirby, no!" Gunther shouted. "I'm sorry! I'm sorry!"

Tracy appeared to smile through bloodstained teeth then lunged for his neck. Gunther cried out as she tore into his flesh with all the aggression of a wild animal.

✝

*H*ill held onto Allison's good arm as she dangled from the vent into the doctor's lounge below. Ellen and Adam caught the little girl and helped her to the floor. Her mother smothered her while sobbing tears of joy. Pricilla hugged both her daughter and granddaughter at the same time. After indulging in the tearful, joyous reunion for a moment, the three within the vent continued on their journey to the linen closet. Crawling through the vent seemed to take longer than it actually did. Monica stopped just above the linen closet and peered through the grate to the room below. Fresh blood stained the excessively white linen piled neatly on the racks. She looked back at her brother and Lexx.

"The closet door is open," she announced softly. "We don't know if any of the infected found their way inside. We'll need to quietly secure that door."

Hill appeared bewildered while staring at his sister. "Lexx closed that door after us, I'm sure of it."

Lexx nodded in agreement.

"Well, it's open now," Monica remarked. "I'll go first, since I'm a little more stealth. You two wait here while I secure the room and barricade that door."

"Be my guest," Hill muttered.

Monica quietly opened the grate, sat on the edge, and then slipped through the opening, dangling from the vent. She dropped nearly silently to the floor, landing in a crouched position. She looked around and at the excessive amount of blood on the linen and quietly headed for the open door. Hill stared through the opening and appeared curious. He looked back at Lexx.

"There wasn't blood in there when we went through, was there?"

"No," Lexx replied. "It was sterile."

Hill appeared concerned and stared through the opening at the blood below. He then looked back at Lexx. "Stay here." He slipped through the opening and landed with less grace than his sister had.

Monica quietly approached the open closet door. Several zombies wandered aimlessly just outside the closet. She reached for the door to close it. A zombie suddenly appeared from alongside the linen rack and lunged for Monica. The male zombie was on top of her too fast for her to fight it. As it tackled her to the floor, she flipped it over her and onto its back. Both ended up inside the corridor among the other zombies. They saw Monica as she scrambled to her feet and lunged for her while snarling. She spun into a high roundhouse kick and nailed the first zombie in the chest, sending it backwards and crashing into a wheelchair lying on the floor. Another zombie came at her from behind. Hill struck the zombie in the chest with the ax, embedding it deep into its chest while knocking it back against the wall. He struggled to pull his ax free while the zombie attempted to reach for him despite the blade within its chest. Hill held the zombie at bay with the ax and reached for his gun. Monica kicked another zombie away from her and saw him going for his gun.

"No," she cried out softly with alarm. "You'll bring them all to this spot."

She turned to fight off another zombie when a second lunged for her and knocked her into the wall. Hill saw the attack and shot the zombie before him. He released the ax and turned to help Monica, prepared to shoot the zombie on her. She kept the first zombie from biting her face while the second zombie went for her arm holding the first one back. Hill shot the zombie about to bite her arm. Monica attempted to get enough distance between her and the zombie pinning her to the wall to fight it, but she had no leverage. The zombie's teeth were now close to her face. A hammer suddenly struck the zombie in the head, spattering thick, dark blood from the wound. She released the zombie and watched it fall to the floor then looked at Lexx holding the bloodied hammer. Nearly a dozen zombies now charged them from the opposite end of the hall. The first of the dozen was nearly on top of them.

"Get into the closet," Monica called out. "I'm right behind you!"

Monica spun into a high roundhouse kick, struck the zombie in the head, and knocked it backwards. A second one was already on top of her. She spun for a return kick and struck it in the chest. The first one recovered more quickly than anticipated, since they didn't respond to pain. She was about to be engulfed by the approaching herd and needed to get away from the two. The first zombie suddenly went down on its right knee. The bone now protruded from its left knee. Lexx stood over the zombie, having broken its knee with a low kick. She plunged the screwdriver through the zombie's ear and yanked it free as it collapsed to the floor. Monica stared with disbelief then turned and karate kicked the one in front of her. As the zombie went down, Hill herded both women into the nearby linen closet. He slammed the door behind them and bolted it. The first few zombies struck the door, unable to stop in time. The second string stepped on the fallen zombies and pawed at the door, attempting to get inside. Inside the linen closet, Hill hurried both women for the dumbwaiter. Monica grabbed Lexx's arm and forced her to face her.

"Where'd you learn that move?" Monica suddenly asked with a look of surprise.

"Med school," she replied simply. "I know every vulnerable place on a person's body. I've also gotten good at resetting bones, so I know just how much force to use to snap them."

Hill appeared sickened. He forced Lexx into the dumbwaiter shaft then turned to Monica. She watched Lexx disappear into the shaft then stared at her brother. Monica attempted to catch her breath then casually indicated Lexx, who was already climbing down the rungs.

"You know," Monica said while panting. "I'm starting to like her. If you don't make a move on her, I just might."

Hill frowned his disapproval to her comment. Monica grinned, although, it was hard to tell if she was serious or just trying to get him going. She climbed into the dumbwaiter shaft. Hill shook his head, muttered a curse, and followed after them.

Chapter Thirty-three

The morgue appeared empty with no signs of life. A faint, repetitive banging was heard from within one of the freezers. It was quickly followed with a series of muffled curses.

"Son-of-a-bitch!" Rolan's faint voice was heard from within freezer six. "I'm going to get my hands on that prick and take his head off!"

There was a moment of silence and possible defeat from the man trapped inside. The freezer door suddenly popped open an inch on its own. Rolan laughed excitedly from his freezer drawer. He kicked open the door and pulled himself out feet first, nearly falling to the floor. He frantically opened several freezer doors while searching for the coroner.

"Doc? Doc?"

Rolan opened one of the doors to reveal Nathan's head. Nathan groaned as Rolan pulled out the slab. He stared up at Rolan with wide, traumatized eyes.

"I never want to do that again," Nathan muttered under his breath. He slowly moved off the slab and shivered more from the creepiness than the cold. "Any other time that freezer opens after two minutes. I was worried the damned latch was actually going to hold for once."

"Thank God for faulty equipment."

Rolan hurried to the counter and slipped into his shoulder holster with his makeshift sling blade. He pulled the sling blade from the holster and wore a look of mayhem on his face.

"We have to help Carson," Rolan announced firmly. "That bastard is armed, so we'll have to get the slip on him. Maybe lure him out somehow."

"I think I know how to lure him out," Nathan announced. "We'll make a little zombie noise. Dr. Sharp will send him out to investigate, and that's when we'll take him out."

"Okay, you've got my vote," Rolan replied.

Nathan routed through one of the drawers, held up a large bone saw, and grinned with all the appeal of a psychopath. "I'm right behind you."

Rolan eyed the bone saw and then the frightening grin on Nathan's face. "No, I'm right behind you, psycho coroner from hell."

†

Lexx, Hill, and Monica hurried across the massive laundry room past the industrial sized washers and toward the main entrance. They had an interesting discussion on their journey down the dumbwaiter shaft. After having filled Monica in on what caused the outbreak, she was suddenly a raging bull--or just a slightly angrier version of her usual self.

"So all these people are infected and Evan and Alpert are dead because of Dr. Sharp?" Monica demanded. The look on her face was frightening.

"The evidence points to him," Hill replied.

"Then you'd better arrest him before I get my hands on him, because I'm going to kill that fucker," Monica snarled as she hurried toward the open laundry room door.

"I know you're upset about your partner and friend, but there won't be any vigilante justice on my watch," Hill informed her sternly.

Monica spun to face Hill with rage, causing him to jump back with surprise. She pointed an accusing finger at him. "Alpert wasn't just a friend!"

There was an awkward silence. Hill frowned and appeared sympathetic toward his sister for the first time. "I'm sorry, Monica," he said gently.

"You're sorry?" she launched back and let a nervous laugh escape. "I had to watch my boyfriend rip out a nurse's throat and then come after me with every intention of tearing me to pieces. Then my partner tried to eat me, and I had to stab him through the eye with a scalpel." She sneered and appeared wildly unpredictable. "It's been a very fucked up day. With the amount of blood on his hands, I don't think anyone's going to shed a tear if I kill the fucker responsible."

"Don't you think I'd like to see him dead for what he's done?" Hill suddenly demanded. "I'm the sheriff, Monica. I have to uphold the law."

"Then you can either take a walk or arrest me after he's dead," she lashed out.

Monica stormed out of the laundry room like a woman with a mission. Lexx walked alongside Hill as they followed her into the corridor.

"Do you think she's serious?" Lexx asked gently while eyeing him.

Hill snorted a laugh. "Yeah, she's serious."

"If anything happens to Carson or Rolan, she may have to stand in line to kill Dr. Sharp," Lexx informed him and hurried to catch up to Monica.

Hill stared after her with surprise. "Great," he muttered, "they finally found something they have in common."

Chapter Thirty-four

While sitting on the whirlpool tub bench within the dimly lit physical therapy room, Carson attempted to control the bleeding wound on Warren's neck. Luckily, there was a first aid kit readily available at the staff desk, but that's where their luck ran out. Carson couldn't stop the wound from bleeding, and the thick, reddish substance was almost caramelized. It was unlike any wound Carson had ever encountered before, although, he wasn't exactly used to dressing wounds on living people. Warren appeared to be in severe discomfort while clinging to his gun like a security blanket. The gun was stained with blood from his hands. He painfully removed the empty clip and inserted a full one. As he cocked the gun, Carson twitched in response. This was, after all, the man who intended to hand Carson over to Dr. Sharp as a test subject. His life clearly didn't matter to Warren. Warren looked at Carson as he finished taping a thick gauze pad to his neck wound. Carson didn't look at him in fear of what was going through the hired killer's mind. In Warren's last fleeting moments, he could potentially end both their lives without a second thought and even rationalize it as the humane thing to do.

"After all I've done to you, you risked your life to help me," Warren gasped softly and shifted with agony. He appeared curious. "Why?"

"Instinct, I suppose," Carson replied without looking at him. "You weren't exactly concerned with my life two minutes earlier. If I would have stopped to think about it, I probably would have let her eat you."

Warren chuckled softly then cringed and handed Carson the gun. "I don't know how long I've got," he informed him. "Make sure you do me before I do you, okay?"

Carson uncertainly took the gun, studied it a moment, and then frowned. He looked back at Warren. "Are we sure it'll come to that?"

"Dr. Sharp couldn't find a cure for the virus, but he was positive saliva to blood was 100% infectious," Warren replied. He grimaced and shifted painfully. "My entire body aches and the wound feels like it's on fire." There was a moment of silence. Warren stared into Carson's eyes with a serious look. "There's no need to wait until I show symptoms, Carson. I'm not a nice person. I don't deserve your mercy."

Carson placed the gun down the back of his pants then studied Warren. "If it's all the same, I'd rather wait until we're sure there's no hope."

"Don't regret that decision," he said while grinning.

"I'll see if the coast is clear," Carson informed him. "I need to get Rolan and Nathan out of those freezers. Once I get them out, I'll come back for you."

Warren managed a slight nod. Carson quickly stood and headed for the door.

"Carson--"

Carson stopped and looked back at Warren sitting on the bench near the whirlpool tub.

"Everything the sheriff needs to know about Dr. Sharp's experiments is in the secretary in his office," Warren informed him. "Including what he gave your uncle."

Carson suddenly appeared alarmed while staring at the dying man several feet away. "Are you saying my uncle could turn into one of those things?"

"I don't know, but I'm surprised he's still alive," Warren replied. "If the treatment he'd received had been successful, he should have woken by now. Just another one of Dr. Gunther Sharp's failures. It's probably best if your uncle passed on. There's no telling what he'll become if he actually wakes."

Carson stared at the man on the bench a long moment. He was obviously disturbed by what he was told. He managed a nod then hurried from the room.

✝

*T*here was a large amount of blood streaked down the hallway leading to the lab. Monica, Hill, and Lexx were alarmed to see blood in the otherwise infection free basement. They followed the blood with shared concern. Something bad had obviously occurred and, judging by the amount of blood, whomever it happened to didn't survive. Lexx was just hoping whatever happened didn't have anything to do with Warren dragging Carson off by gunpoint. There was a thump coming from the lab down the hall. Hill and Lexx clutched their weapons as they approached the lab. Monica showed little hesitation while reaching for the door and slowly opened it. Rolan suddenly lunged out the door at her with his sling blade prepared to strike. Monica blocked the weapon, jabbed Rolan in the abdomen, and flipped him over her and onto his back. Rolan groaned loudly. Lexx let out a startled scream, dropped her weapon, and leaped to Rolan's side. Nathan stood in the lab doorway and stared at them with a look of surprise on his face.

"Oh, Rolan," Lexx gasped. "Are you okay?"

"Hey, Lexx," he managed a soft groan then smiled. "Who's your friend? She's cute."

It was only a few minutes later when they had assembled in the lab. Monica looked from the bloodstained laboratory to Nathan at the counter peering into the microscope. Rolan continued to rub his sore back and glared at Monica. She caught his stare and showed little remorse for her 'shock and awe' on him.

"I said I was sorry," Monica snorted.

"I believe you called me an idiot for startling you," Rolan remarked with annoyance, "but I'm pretty sure you never said you were sorry."

Monica rolled her eyes, folded her arms across her chest, and walked away. "Whatever--"

"We need to find Carson," Lexx informed them demandingly. "After that scene in the hallway, there's no telling what happened to him."

"If that was his blood in the hallway, trust me, you don't want to find him," Monica remarked lowly.

"Monica," Hill scolded.

"Oh, give it up, Hill," Monica snapped at her brother and indicated Lexx with a wave of her hand. "She's obviously not interested in you, so stop kissing her ass and focus on doing your job."

All eyes were suddenly on Hill. Lexx was curious as to why Monica had made that assumption. Did she sense something in her brother's actions? Lexx usually knew what Carson was thinking just by observing his actions. Of course, Carson wasn't exactly difficult to read. Hill appeared embarrassed, turned, and took a few steps away from them while passing his sister.

He leaned closer to her and muttered, "If we get out of this, I'm kicking your ass."

Monica challenged him with a look. Lexx watched the exchange between brother and sister, instantly being reminded of her and Carson. They were no different. Lexx paced the room while waiting for confirmation of Nathan's findings on the blood he was examining. She leaned against the far wall and watched the men talk quietly over the counter. For once, she wasn't interested in their conversation. She felt they should be out looking for Carson, in case he was still alive. Monica approached Lexx and casually leaned against the wall near her. The woman pretended to be disinterested, but Lexx suspected she had an agenda the moment she walked over.

"He likes you, you know that," Monica gently informed her without taking her eyes off the men at the counter.

"Who?" Lexx asked.

Monica glared at her. "Who do you think?" she snapped. "Hill." She frowned and looked away. "I can see it by the way he looks at you. He's a good guy." She hesitated. "It's none of my business, but if you're not interested, you need to shoot him down right away. He's a bit of a hopeless romantic and tends to get ahead of himself."

"You think he's interested in me?" Lexx suddenly asked and appeared curious. "I wouldn't think I'm his type."

Monica suddenly glared at her with surprise. "You're absolutely his type." She snorted a humored laugh. "Do you think he's interested in girly girls like Dr. Kirby?"

Lexx shifted uncomfortably. "It had crossed my mind. What man wouldn't want someone like her?"

"My brother," she replied simply. "He's not into high-maintenance women. Besides, Dr. Kirby used to date his best friend.

She broke his heart, and he moved away to forget about her. Hill never forgave her for chasing away his best friend like that." Monica studied Lexx and gave her a serious look. "You like him, don't you?"

Lexx considered and held back her smile. "I really hadn't given it much thought."

Monica stared at her a moment then grinned. "Uh, huh," she remarked. "Next time you want to tell a convincing lie, try saying it with a straight face, okay?"

Lexx looked at Monica. They exchanged smiles for the first time. Nathan continued to stare into the microscope then straightened and looked back at the others.

"It wasn't Carson's blood," Nathan informed them. "Whoever was attacked had already been infected long before the hallway incident."

"It couldn't have been Dr. Kirby," Lexx boldly announced and hurried across the room toward him and the counter. "Even if that blood was infected, I could tell it was from a living person not a dead one."

"So Carson could still be alive?" Rolan asked.

"There's nothing to indicate otherwise," Nathan informed them with renewed hope.

Rolan and Lexx appeared relieved.

"We need to find him," Lexx announced and looked at the sheriff.

Hill stared back at Lexx then caught his sister's glare as she approached them. Monica folded her arms across her chest and raised her brows in silent question. He obviously knew exactly what she was expressing with that look. Hill ignored his sister and focused his attention on Lexx and their current dilemma.

"We'll do a sweep of the basement," Hill announced firmly then looked at the others.

Monica groaned and looked away.

"If the blood in the corridor contains infection," Nathan announced, "then that means it's not just Dr. Kirby we need to worry about. Someone else has been infected."

"There's also the hired goon," Hill remarked. "If he wasn't the one who bled out, that means he's still a potential threat. Carson could be hiding from him, so we can't go out there announcing ourselves."

They all nodded in agreement. Hill looked back at Monica and appeared curious.

"Do you intend to help us?" he demanded impatiently.

"How crazy do you think I am?" she blurted out and appeared annoyed by the question. "Mom will kill me if I let anything happen to your lazy ass."

"I'll take that in the spirit it was intended," Hill muttered while rolling his eyes.

Chapter Thirty-five

Carson stood within the empty morgue and opened several freezer doors. He looked more frustrated with each freezer that didn't contain his friends. The phone rang, startling him. Carson lunged for the phone and didn't even wait to hear the person's voice on the other end.

"Lexx?" he gasped then immediately appeared disappointed. "Oh, I was expecting a call from someone else." He hesitated then seemed enthusiastic. "Really? That's great." There was another pause. He suddenly looked concerned. "What? You're kidding, right? No, that's not so great." There was another pause. "Thanks for the update. I have to go."

Carson hung up the phone with the concern evident on his face and hurried for the door. He opened the door to see Warren with a glazed over look in his eyes. Carson screamed and fumbled with the gun down the back of his pants. Warren bared his teeth and tackled him across the room and into the exam table. The gun flew from his hand as he attempted to keep Warren from biting him. Warren's bared teeth came close to his face, and Carson was losing the battle.

Hill and Nathan suddenly appeared in the morgue and pulled Warren off him. They cast Warren across the room, disorientating him only momentarily. He lunged for Rolan. Rolan swung his makeshift sling blade and sliced through the dead man's neck with ease, decapitating Warren. As Warren's head was thrown across the room, Lexx grabbed Hill and cried out. The head rolled across the floor and stopped near Monica's booted feet. She stared at the severed head then casually looked at Rolan.

"Nicely done," Monica announced a little too proudly.

Carson grabbed the discarded gun and looked at them with concern. Although happy to see them, he seemed preoccupied. "The nurse on Brandon's floor just called," he announced in rushed speech. "One of your deputies leaked word that CDC was going to do a clean sweep of the entire first floor. They're calling the emergency room a total loss."

"Clean sweep?" Lexx gasped and looked at Hill. "Does that mean--?"

"Yeah, they're going to kill anything that moves," Hill replied and appeared deep in thought.

"They can't do that," Monica suddenly proclaimed with hostility. "There are survivors in the doctor's lounge. They're not infected. I made sure of that."

"Trust me, they won't stop to ask," Carson muttered under his breath.

"No, they're my responsibility. I kept them safe," she lashed out. "I told them to stay there until help arrived. I left them there to be slaughtered!"

"How much time?" Hill asked Carson.

"Fifteen minutes at most."

"You can't seriously be thinking about going back up there," Nathan suddenly announced. "That badge isn't going to mean squat to those guys. They're playing for keeps."

"And if they discover the blood and one single infected body down here, they're going to do the same to us," Lexx informed the others.

"She's right," Nathan agreed.

"We need to move to another floor, before they exterminate us as well," Lexx announced.

Hill considered their comments only a moment then quickly looked around the room. "Okay, we'll go up the shaft to another floor. We need to leave any blood-covered clothing down here." He seemed to consider more options. "I saw some clean scrub suits in the laundry room. We'll slip into those and blend in with the rest of the staff." He glanced at his sister and her unpredictable expression then looked back at the others. "Monica and I are going for the survivors in the doctor's lounge."

†

All six hurried across the laundry room with their makeshift weapons. Time was running out for any survivors on the first floor. Hill stopped them near the mounted wall phone. Hill indicated the phone to Nathan.

"Call the doctor's lounge and tell them to get into the ventilation ducks. They have to make certain there's nothing to indicate they went up there. We can't have CDC thinking the infection traveled to another floor," Hill announced sternly. "Tell them that Monica and I are on our way to help them." He glanced at the others. "Carson and Rolan will secure clean scrub uniforms for all of us."

Carson and Rolan hurried across the laundry room just beyond the industrial sized washing machines to where the clean scrub uniforms were stacked. Monica and Hill ran after them and for the dumbwaiter. Lexx and Nathan approached the wall phone between the freight elevator and the laundry entrance. Nathan punched in the number for the doctor's lounge. Before he had a chance to speak, the freight elevator dinged. Nathan and Lexx froze simultaneously and looked at the elevator with shared concern. Hill and Monica suddenly stopped halfway across the laundry room to the sound and looked back as the doors opened. Ten zombies poured out of the elevator and charged for Nathan and Lexx. Nathan pushed Lexx toward the main laundry room door. Hill and Monica stared with shared looks of horror as the horde of zombies chased after them. Hill turned to Monica.

"Go to the doctor's lounge and take the survivors upstairs," he quickly announced. "I need to help them."

Hill ran across the laundry room without awaiting her response. Monica appeared alarmed and stared after him.

"Hill! No!" Monica cried out.

Monica watched him head for the door without indicating he'd heard her. She cursed softly and ran for the dumbwaiter around the corner. She approached Carson and Rolan, who stacked several scrub uniforms then hastily changed into their own. Carson eyed her as he pulled the scrub top over his head.

"Where's Lexx?" Carson asked.

"She's with Nathan and Hill," she quickly replied without looking at them. "They'll be along shortly. The two of you need to go now."

"You're going to the E.R. break room alone?" Rolan suddenly asked.

"I'll be fine," she insisted. "Just go."

"No, I'll go with you," Rolan informed her. "I'm stronger than I look. I can help lift people into the vents."

"I don't have time to argue," Monica remarked and grabbed a sack full of clean scrub uniforms. She tossed the sack over her back and climbed into the dumbwaiter shaft. Carson and Rolan exchanged looks and hurried through the small opening after her.

Chapter Thirty-six

$\mathcal{T}$he eight survivors sat quietly around the doctor's lounge. They had moved the dead bodies toward the back and covered them. A few survivors talked softly between themselves. Pricilla held her granddaughter on her lap. The little girl flipped through a golf magazine and asked many questions about golf. She wanted to know why so many of the magazines were about the sport. Ellen brought two cups of coffee and some hot chocolate to them where they sat. The zombie was still heard thumping around inside the shower room beyond the locker room. Ellen jumped at nearly every sound the zombie made. It was unsettling knowing there was one inside the shower room with only a thin door between them and it. Adam now paced the room while occasionally looking up to the closed vent above them. They hadn't seen Monica in over an hour. There was some concern that she may have abandoned them, but even more concern that something got to her first.

Sounds from the shower room finally subsided, leaving the doctor's lounge unusually quiet for the first time. It was a relief not to hear the relentless thumping, but the silence was almost unsettling.

Pricilla finally looked up. She obviously didn't like the newly found silence.

"Do you think someone should check on our friend?" she asked while raising a skeptical brow.

Allison looked at her grandmother. "If he's our friend, why is he locked in that room?"

"It's an expression, dear," Ellen replied softly.

"I thought he was in a time out," Allison announced casually while paging through her magazine. "Like daddy."

Ellen and Pricilla gave the little girl odd looks. "What do you mean 'like daddy'?" her mother asked.

"Lexx said Daddy had to stay locked up until he was ready to play nice," she announced. "In the place we were staying. Where I got my cast."

"You saw your father?" Pricilla suddenly asked.

Allison nodded. "Yeah, he was locked in the nurse's area," she replied. "Lexx said he needed to stay in there, because he wasn't playing nice."

Pricilla and Ellen exchanged uncomfortable looks. Neither was prepared to tell her the cold, cruel truth just yet. Adam continued his pacing, turned, and nearly collided with the zombie from the shower room. He stared at the male zombie with flesh torn from its shoulder and part of its intestines hanging out like a beer belly. For a moment, Adam could only stare blankly into the zombie's dead eyes. Everyone suddenly screamed. The zombie lunged for Adam. Adam stepped out of its path and gave it a toss for added measure. The zombie lost its balance and stumbled into the nearby wall. Everyone scattered to avoid the unstable infected man. Moans and snarls were now heard from outside the doctor's lounge door. The zombie lunged for Ellen, who bolted from its path, leading it away from her daughter and mother. Pricilla leaped from her chair, pulled Allison further across the breakroom, and forced her to stand behind her as she held the crutch in her hands.

The zombie lunged for the nurse. She attempted to escape, but it grabbed her arm. As she struggled to pull her arm free, Adam grabbed the nearby fire extinguisher and ran up behind the zombie. He struck it on the head just as it bit the nurse on the lower arm. She screamed as the zombie took a chunk of flesh from her arm. Before it had a chance to enjoy its treat, the zombie was thrown sideways from the fire extinguisher striking its head. Despite a large flap of scalp hanging from the side of its head, the zombie turned and charged for Adam. It tackled Adam to the sofa and attempted to bite his face. Adam cried out and held the zombie back while attempting to keep its teeth from tearing into his arm. Pricilla struck the zombie in the head several times with the crutch to keep it from biting Adam, but she couldn't get much leverage on the hard angle. She didn't want to throw the zombie's snapping teeth closer to Adam's face by accident.

Adam finally managed to throw the zombie off him. The zombie crashed to the floor. As Adam attempted to jump off the sofa, the zombie grabbed his foot and bit his ankle below his pants. Adam screamed as the zombie's teeth tore into his leg, saturating his lower pants leg with blood. Pricilla struck the zombie in the head several times with a better angle and more force, knocking the zombie away from Adam. The injured man pulled himself away from the fallen zombie and allowed the bleeding nurse to help him to his feet. The zombie attempted to return to its feet with less coordination. Pricilla struck the zombie in the head again with the crutch, but it still made it to its feet. She went for another swing when the zombie lunged for her and tackled her to the floor. The zombie was on top of her and came at her face with its bloodstained teeth. Pricilla screamed and grabbed for her discarded crutch. The zombie bit down on a pink cast. The hideous crunching sound of its teeth breaking off echoed through the room. The zombie pulled back and snarled at Allison, who was crouched alongside her grandmother with her pink cast in front of her face protecting her.

Despite having lost its front teeth, the zombie lunged for Allison, who screamed shrill and loud. The crutch slammed into the zombie's face, ramming its nose back and into its brain. The zombie was motionless a moment then collapsed to the floor. Pricilla and Allison looked back to see Ellen holding the bloodstained crutch while she panted heavily. She tossed the crutch aside and helped pull them to their feet. The sound of several zombies pounding on the lounge door was now heard. All the commotion from the doctor's lounge had alerted them to the delicious entrees inside. The door began to vibrate. There had to be at least a dozen of them pounding against the door in order to vibrate it. There was a good chance the lock wasn't going to hold. The three non-injured men ran to the door to help brace it shut.

Pricilla and Ellen looked at Adam then to the large amount of blood covering the bottom of his pants and his shoe. He clutched his ankle in agony while leaning against the wall for support. The nurse held a cloth around her lower arm, but it was already bleeding through. Their injuries were serious enough that they would undoubtedly turn in less than an hour from the infection. Adam met Pricilla's sympathetic gaze.

He frowned and defiantly shook his head. "No, don't feel sorry for me," Adam boldly announced and straightened proudly. "You were right. We should have dealt with him when we had the chance."

There was an awkward silence as he stared at her while reaching into his pocket. Pricilla appeared curious and attempted to see what was in his hand. By the time she saw the pocketknife, he was already plunging it through the nurse's ear and into her brain. She gasped only briefly and immediately dropped to the floor. Ellen and Allison screamed. Ellen pulled her daughter's face into her chest and shielded her from the gruesome image. Pricilla just stared at Adam with shock.

He offered a tiny smile and gave her a polite nod. "I won't make the same mistake twice," Adam informed her.

Without a moment's hesitation, he plunged the pocketknife deep into his own ear. He instantly dropped to the floor, blood spilling from his ear. Pricilla shut her eyes and groaned softly.

Chapter Thirty-seven

Lexx and Nathan ran across the maintenance shop with several zombies gaining on them. As they ran, Nathan pointed to the vent opening on the ceiling nearly fifteen feet above them. There was no visible access to the vent. He pushed her toward some metal shelves near the back. Lexx quickly scaled the cluttered shelf with Nathan just behind her. She reached the top shelf, turned on her hands and knees, and extended her hand to Nathan. Less inclined to climb, the zombies pushed on the shelf to get to them, causing it to sway. Lexx appeared alarmed, gasped, and held onto the edge of the smooth metal shelf. Nathan looked below him at the zombies as they reached for him and rocked the shelf. It wouldn't be long before the shelf toppled with them on it.

He looked back at Lexx. "Go! Across the shelves to the vent," Nathan ordered.

She suddenly looked at him with horror on her face. "What about you?"

He offered a tiny smile. "I'm the diversion."

Lexx's eyes widened as she stared at him and the strange smile on his face. "Nathan, no!"

"I know what I'm doing, Lexx," he informed her. "If I stay, we're both going to die. I can buy you enough time to reach the vent."

"Nathan--"

Nathan offered her a knowing smile and, before she could protest, leaped off the shelf. He landed on top of a female zombie, tackling her to the floor. He scrambled off her and sprang to his feet before the others could pile on top of him.

"Go, Lexx!" he cried out then yelled to the zombies, "Hey, come and get me!"

She felt some hope for his survival after watching his quick reflexes. The zombies chased Nathan leaving only two behind still intent on reaching Lexx. The shelf no longer swayed. Lexx cursed and quickly crawled along the top of the shelf, throwing a few items at the zombies below as she made her way to the vent. She looked back to check on Nathan's progress. To her horror, there was a pile of eight zombies against the back wall. Lexx cursed softly, fought her tears, and continued for the vent. The two remaining zombies followed her from the ground and clawed at the shelves despite her throwing objects at them. She reached the end of the shelf and looked at the pipes along the ceiling near the vent several feet out of her reach. She looked down to the relentless zombies below her. There were only two, but it wouldn't be long before the other eight finished their snack and returned for her. She took a deep breath and concentrated on her best approach to cross the pipe. Thinking like a monkey would be to her advantage at the moment.

†

Soldiers and CDC in hazmat uniforms stormed through the broken emergency waiting room door just a little before dawn. The remaining zombies within the waiting room charged the armed soldiers, who immediately opened fire. They took several body shots but continued charging for the armed men. It only took them a moment or two to realize they needed to shoot them in the head in order to keep them down permanently. They continued into the emergency room corridor, shooting anything that moved. After a small section was cleared, a man appeared from one of the exam rooms with his hands in the air and relief on his weary face.

"Thank God," he cried out cheerfully. "Am I glad to see you guys!"

Without hesitation, CDC shot the man with several rounds. His body jerked and jolted from the bullets riddling his body before he finally collapsed to the floor in a bloody heap. The soldiers and CDC continued along the hall. More zombies began appearing and ran for them. The gunfire continued.

†

*P*ricilla, Ellen and Allison stood near the back of the doctor's lounge and watched in horror as the remaining three men from their group attempted to hold the busted door closed. Zombies groaned and thumped against the thick door. The lock was already dangling with fragments of wood still attached to it. It wouldn't be long before they plowed their way through as the three men were quickly losing energy. The vent grate flew open, startling the three women toward the back. The men holding the door closed were too busy to bother looking. Monica dropped through the opening and landed gracefully on the floor. Rolan jumped down behind her with less grace and a lot of grunting.

"They're getting through," one of the men holding the door shouted to Monica.

Nathan's phone call never got through, so they had no idea what was about to unfold outside the lounge or how much danger they were actually facing. They had no idea that the zombies were no longer their biggest threat.

"In the vent!" Monica ordered while pointing.

The faint sound of assault rifles were heard being fired from deep within the emergency room. The others appeared hopeful and clung to one another with anticipation.

"Listen," Ellen cried out with glee. "They're coming to rescue us!"

"That's not the sound of a rescue," Rolan informed them while becoming increasingly anxious. He grabbed a chair and placed it beneath the opening in the ceiling. "That's the sound of extermination. They're going to shoot anyone on this floor whether you're infected or not. Now get in the vent!"

They didn't appear convinced and exchanged looks rather than springing into action. Rolan forcibly grabbed Ellen, startling her, and hoisted her onto the chair beneath the vent. She reluctantly did as he ordered, given little choice as he grabbed her buttocks in both hands and thrust her upward toward the vent. As Rolan pushed more people onto the chair and through the vent, Monica and another man pushed the vending machine in front of the door. It fell in front of the door with a thunderous crash. The door vibrated and harshly struck the vending machine. There were enough zombies behind the door that they were pushing the vending machine a little at a time with each thrust. It made a hideous metallic scraping sound as it dug into the floor, leaving a deep scratch in the tile.

"We don't have much time," Monica informed Rolan, now feeling the pressure.

The sound of automatic weapons firing was getting closer and would soon be upon them. Rolan pushed the last man onto the chair then turned to Monica and motioned for her while she kept her weight against the vending machine to keep it stable. They'd pushed it far enough away from the doorframe that it would easily topple with the right amount of force.

Rolan stood by the chair and extended his hand to her. "Come on!"

She looked back at him and his extended hand. She nervously shook her head. "Once I let go, we're only going to have a few seconds before they push through," Monica informed him. "You can't wait for me."

"I'm sure as hell not leaving you!"

The sound of gunfire was now in the corridor outside their lounge. There was a thunderous commotion within the corridor, although it didn't stop the relentless zombies from pushing on the door. Several zombies' reached into the room past the vending machine and attempted to grab Monica.

"Come on," Rolan shouted. "Get your ass up there!"

"I'm right behind you," she called back then assessed the height of the vent and the chair beneath it. She gave him a quick, concerning look. "Give me some room up there! I'll be coming in hot!"

Rolan nodded and hoisted himself into the vent. Monica kept her weight against the vending machine, took a few deep breaths, and then bolted for the chair below the vent. There was a thunderous crash as the vending machine toppled and clipped Monica's leg. She was thrown across the room and to the floor. She clutched her lower leg and cried out in agony. The zombies pushed past the vending machine. Monica attempted to move to her feet but could barely stand. As she made it to her feet, she stared helplessly as Alpert lunged for her while the others attempted to push past the vending machine. A screwdriver was suddenly plunged through Alpert's eye, and he fell to the floor. Monica looked back at Rolan, who now stood alongside her. Rolan swiftly pulled his makeshift sling blade from his holster and swung for the second zombie, slicing its head in two.

He dropped the stick, grabbed Monica by the waist, and hoisted her up to the vent. She grabbed onto the vent and pulled herself through while Rolan pushed her from below with a tremendous thrust. She cried out in agony to her broken leg but continued into the vent with determination. More zombies began to push their way into the room. Rolan reclaimed his stick and lunged for the approaching zombie. He struck it in the chest with the sling blade and pushed it into the others, throwing them backwards. Rolan tossed his sling blade, ran for the chair, and leaped up to the vent while purposely toppling the chair behind him. He hoisted himself into the vent. A zombie grabbed his dangling leg and attempted to bite it. Rolan kicked the zombie in the face as he pulled his legs the rest of the way into the vent.

The vent grate closed just as soldiers crashed through the door. Without hesitation or even checking their targets, they sprayed the room with bullets. It wouldn't have mattered if there had been any survivors. The soldiers weren't looking for any.

Chapter Thirty-eight

Lexx grabbed onto the pipe on the ceiling above her while keeping her knees on the shelf and again looked at the two zombies below. They watched her and waited. She was concerned that they seemed convinced she would fall into their laps. It didn't help boost her confidence any. Lexx wrapped her ankles around the pipe and shimmied slowly across it while hanging upside down. She inched her way toward the vent. The smooth metal made sliding her legs easy, but she constantly felt as if she was about to lose her grip with her arms. The zombies followed and reached for her despite several feet separating them. Lexx reached the vent and attempted to open the grate. It didn't budge. She groaned with disgust. It just wasn't her day. She clung to the pipe with one arm and her legs while carefully removing a screwdriver from her holster. She poked at the grate, hoping to jolt it loose. The pipe suddenly groaned beneath her weight. Lexx gasped and looked along the pipe behind her. The pipe was starting to bow and water leaked from a break along a carelessly soldered joint. She shut her eyes and groaned.

"Oh hell--"

The pipe suddenly broke. Lexx released her ankles and allowed herself to drop rather than fall. She managed to land on her feet then fell to the floor. The two zombies immediately pounced on her. Lexx screamed and attempted to hold the first zombie back and keep it from biting her. Unfortunately, the second zombie went for her legs. As she kicked at the second zombie while holding the first away from her face, she felt the morbid realization that she was about to be eaten alive. She often thought being eaten by an alligator had to be the worst way to die, but she somehow felt she was about to be proved wrong. A gunshot suddenly rang out, startling her. The zombie by her legs was thrown off and slowly recovered. Hill kicked the zombie on top of her in the head, sending it flying across the floor. Both zombies returned to their feet and lunged for them. Hill shot both in the head without hesitation. They both dropped to the floor and didn't get back up. He took her hand and pulled her to her feet. He never looked as good to her as he did at that moment. And if it weren't for the zombies from the back of the shop running for them, she almost certainly would have kissed him. Hill pushed her toward the main door.

"Time to go!" he shouted.

Lexx and Hill ran along the corridor with the eight remaining zombies close behind. They made it to the laundry room and darted inside. Hill slammed the door behind them and braced the door shut with his spade on a stick. He hurried her toward the dumbwaiter on the other end of the laundry room. They grabbed scrub uniforms from the nearby shelf and tossed them into the shaft. Hill pushed Lexx to the opening. She quickly climbed into the shaft. Gunther suddenly appeared and tackled Hill against the wall. Lexx looked out from the shaft opening and screamed as Gunther attempted to bite the sheriff. Hill held Gunther back while reaching for his holstered weapon. Lexx climbed out of the shaft in an effort to help and suddenly came face-to-face with Tracy.

The naked woman stood before her and snarled through bloodstained teeth. Lexx stared at Tracy with horror. Hill appeared to be losing the battle against Gunther, who attempted to bite his throat. Lexx kicked Tracy high and hard in the chest, sending the naked woman backwards into Gunther. All three, including Hill, were thrown to the floor. Hill scrambled out from under Gunther. Lexx grabbed his arm and pulled him to his feet. Gunther grabbed his leg and attempted to bite it. Hill removed his gun, aimed it at Gunther's head, and pulled the trigger. It clicked empty. Hill gasped with alarm then thrust his leg back and attempted to kick Gunther in order to free his leg, but he kept a tight grip on his pants leg. Lexx released Hill and kicked Gunther in the face, sending him backwards, and snapping his jaw. His lower jaw flopped inside his skin with nothing to hold it in place. Tracy was now on her feet and lunged for Lexx. She tackled her into a nearby linen cart, toppling the cart and covering both with dirty linen. Hill was alarmed by the large mass moving around beneath the linen. There was no telling who was where.

"Lexx!" he cried out while frantically pulling linen from the massive pile and tossing it aside.

The large mass of linen was suddenly propelled backwards and into him. Both crashed to the floor. Hill scrambled out from beneath the massive pile of sheets and sprang to his feet, uncertain if that was Lexx or not. Gunther suddenly jumped on Hill's back and attempted to bite the side of his neck, despite his flopping lower jaw. Hill flipped the zombie doctor over his shoulder and onto the moving mass of linen. There was a loud crunch. He jumped back with surprise. The pile no longer moved beneath Gunther's thrashing body. Lexx jumped up from the pile of linen near the cart and looked around while breathing heavily.

"Where is she?"

He appeared relieved to see her then indicated the mass beneath Gunther, who slowly moved to his feet. Both heard the sound of automatic weapons being fired just outside the room. Even more so than being attacked by ravenous undead, they feared the approaching CDC more.

"We need to go!" Hill cried out and indicated the dumbwaiter behind them.

"If Gunther tries to get into the shaft, they'll know someone went in there," she announced with panic in her voice.

Concern swept over Hill, because he knew she was right. Hill took a step back from the doctor, who was nearly to his feet. He snap kicked him under the chin with all his energy. Gunther flew upward and then backwards. He landed on his back near the linen rack. Hill removed a pen from his pocket and rammed it into Gunther's eye. Lexx immediately cringed. Gunther still twitched. Hill promptly stomped on the remaining pen sticking out of his eye, driving the pen deep into his brain. Gunther finally stopped moving. The gunfire outside the laundry room door ceased. Panic filled Lexx as she grabbed Hill's arm.

"Go! Go!" Lexx cried out with terror.

Lexx pushed Hill toward the dumbwaiter shaft. Both climbed inside and shut the door behind them. The door to the laundry room burst open with a loud crash. CDC with their automatic weapons filtered into the room and swept it for any infected. The mass moved from beneath the pile of dirty linen. One of the armed men sprayed a barrage of bullets into the pile of linen. The mass no longer moved. The CDC soldier then looked at Gunther's dead body with a pen drilled deep into his eye. The soldier appeared curious and looked around the area.

Chapter Thirty-nine

$\mathcal{T}$he CDC, dressed in masks and sterile suits, stormed through the second floor hallway alongside soldiers. All were heavily armed with assault rifles. Their appearance was frightening to the survivors on the second floor. The nurses and visitors appeared horrified and watched silently as they entered each room, checking for any remaining infected people. Two CDC soldiers entered the room near the linen closet with their weapons raised. Rolan and Carson stood on either side of the occupied hospital bed, dressed in green scrub uniforms, and pretended to care for their patient, who looked a lot like Monica in a hospital gown. Rolan appeared alarmed to see the men with automatic weapons. Monica lie in the hospital bed beneath the covers with her eyes closed. Carson took Monica's pulse with his thumb to her inner wrist and ignored the men. The soldiers looked around then left the room. Both men groaned softly and allowed their bodies to sag in response. Monica opened her eyes and glared at Carson.

"Hey, idiot," she snapped hotly. "You don't take a person's pulse with your thumb. You're lucky they didn't notice or are dumber than they look."

Carson forced an embarrassed smile then collapsed into a nearby chair and groaned. Rolan sat on Monica's bedside with the same look of exhaustion.

"I hope Lexx and Hill made it out," Carson said softly while scratching his temple.

"If they get caught, CDC will probably destroy the entire hospital as a precaution," Rolan informed him.

Carson stared at Rolan and appeared alarmed.

"I was joking," Rolan announced with a grin. His joke wasn't appreciated. He gently cleared his throat then looked at Monica, who struggled to sit up. "How's your leg?"

"Fractured, I'm sure, but I'll live," she remarked then looked at him and held her breath. "Thanks for coming back for me. It was very stupid of you."

"You're welcome, you ungrateful bitch," Rolan replied while hiding his smile.

"Don't read too much into this--" Monica announced then grabbed his shirt, pulled him toward her, and kissed him quickly on the lips.

As she broke off the kiss, Rolan smiled with embarrassment. Carson rolled his eyes and looked away.

†

Two soldiers in sterile suits and masks burst into the linen closet with their weapons raised. Hill had Lexx pressed up against the linen rack with her leg up on his hip while they aggressively kissed and groped each other. Both wore their illegally obtained scrub uniforms and looked the part of hospital workers. Lexx saw the men, gasped with surprise, and attempted to pull away from Hill. He didn't release her and kissed her neck and throat instead. Lexx nudged him harshly while nervously grinning at the soldiers with their weapons aimed. Hill pulled away from her, saw the intimidating weapons, and appeared alarmed.

"This isn't how it looks," Hill announced defensively while holding his hands in the air. "She had something in her eye. I was just trying to get it out for her."

The soldiers shook their heads with disgust and left the linen closet. Lexx and Hill sighed with relief and clung to each other. Both laughed nervously. Lexx sank against Hill, rested her head on his shoulder, and groaned softly.

"That was close," Lexx muttered.

"Too close," he replied and nuzzled her head with his cheek while grinning. "Another couple of minutes and you wouldn't have been able to pry me off you."

Lexx pulled back, eyed him with surprise, and then laughed softly. "You're absolutely terrible," she announced firmly. A tiny smile crossed her face as she smoothed his scrub top. "At least let me shower first."

Hill stared at her with surprise to the comment. He smiled lustfully and again pulled her against him. "I'll reserve us a shower for two at my place."

She laughed softly, clung to him, and stared into his ice blue eyes. There was no way she would refuse that offer. After the night they had, she wanted some quality time in the bedroom with this man.

"I may be looking forward to it more than you," she said while smiling deviously.

Hill suddenly laughed while clinging to her. "Doubtful, but I appreciate the enthusiasm."

He kissed her passionately and aggressively. She immediately returned the kiss and sank into his arms.

Chapter Forty

$\mathcal{I}$t was later that same afternoon by the time CDC had finished operation clean sweep and were aggressively working on bagging the massive number of infected bodies. They cleaned and sterilized a lot of the hospital, removing all body parts and any bloody clothing and furniture they came across. Their efficiency was concerning, almost as if they'd done this sort of thing many times in the past. The emergency room remained off limits as the cleanup continued. It would take them most of that following night to finish their work in the large area covered with infection. The basement was declared clean, since it contained less infection than the first floor, and essential hospital personnel were allowed to return to most areas. Voices were heard arguing within the corridor just outside the morgue door. Carson and Rolan pushed a stretcher into the morgue while Lexx shook her head with disgust and held the door open for them.

"I can't believe you asked her out," Lexx remarked with annoyance.

"Hey, just because you don't get along--" Rolan snapped and decided against finishing the sentence.

"That's an understatement," Carson muttered. "Personally, I think that woman is scary."

"Besides, she turned me down anyway," Rolan pouted. His look immediately turned demanding. "And you should talk. I saw that kiss you gave Sheriff Burke when he dropped you off earlier. You can't tell me you and the sheriff weren't getting freaky at his place. You were gone all morning and half the afternoon."

Lexx hid her lustful smile and avoided looking at them. "Can we argue about this later? I'd like to collect our client and get out of here. There's no telling how long before CDC changes their mind and sanitizes the entire building with us in it."

"I'm all for getting out of here," Rolan announced. "I wasn't exactly thrilled coming back here in the first place. All those burning bodies in the incinerator gives me the creeps. And I'm not easily creeped."

"After all we've been through; I can't believe you're acting so nervous," Carson remarked as he approached the freezers. "Me, I'm feeling invincible for the first time. Surviving last night toughened me. Nothing scares me anymore."

Carson casually opened one of the freezer doors. Two hands suddenly appeared from the freezer, grabbed the edges by the opening, and thrust the metal slab from the freezer. Carson cried out and threw himself against the wall. Nathan sat up on the slab and shivered.

"Damn that's cold!" Nathan cried out and slowly pulled himself to his feet.

Lexx was stunned to see him then turned enthusiastic. She laughed and hugged him. "You made it! I thought you were dead for sure!"

He chuckled softly and enjoyed her warm embrace while shivering. "I was a linebacker in high school, remember?" he informed her through chattering teeth and finally pulled away to meet her gaze. "I plowed right through those bastards. They never knew what hit them."

Lexx found a blanket and placed it over his shoulders. She couldn't believe his survived. It didn't seem possible. "But I saw them piling up on someone, didn't I?"

"I escaped through a storage cubby," he announced. "I was able to make my way through the clutter and into physical therapy. By the time I got there, I heard gunshots, so I came back here and locked myself in that freezer. Even though I turned the freezer off, it still gets pretty cold in there, but I figured I'd rather take my chances not being found for a few days over being shot by my friends at CDC."

"Yeah, we met a few of your friends from CDC," Rolan casually informed Nathan. "I'd say we're lucky to have survived the experience."

†

Carson stood alongside the secretary within Dr. Sharp's office early that evening while Hill removed the notebook from the metal case. Carson peered over his shoulder as Hill scanned through the notebook. He stopped his finger on Brandon's name near the bottom of the page. They exchanged concerned looks. Hill took a deep breath, removed a pen from his pocket, and scratched out Brandon's name. He wrote 'deceased' behind it then replaced the notebook and looked at Carson.

"Okay?"

Carson frowned and nodded. "Thanks, Hill."

"Are you sure you don't want to tell Lexx what Warren said on his deathbed?"

"No," he replied gently. "I don't want to upset her unnecessarily. She already knows Dr. Sharp injected one of his drugs into Brandon's system. Nathan will continue to take blood samples and monitor his condition." Carson drew a deep breath and held it. "At least we know he wasn't injected with the same toxin that reanimated Tracy. We'll worry about side effects in the event he pulls out of the coma."

Hill nodded. "Okay, that's your call," he announced. "As long as Nathan is monitoring the situation."

"He's willing to go along with it," Carson replied. "For Lexx's sake."

†

It was two days later and things in their little town had finally returned to normal or something close enough to normal. CDC remained in town the entire two days but finally left that morning. The reminders of the undead invasion to their small town would remain with them a long time with countless people dead and

187

burned in the incinerator. The hospital seemed to be back to business as usual, although security had been excessively tight in the days following the cleanup. Several specialists had closed their offices on the fifth floor and looked to open their practices elsewhere, preferably in another town. No one really blamed them for their decision to pull out.

Lexx was once again in Brandon's room on the fourth floor ICU. She slept with her head on his shoulder while clinging to his arm. He still remained unresponsive in his comatose state. There was no telling if and when he'd ever come out of it or what his condition would be when he did. By her eye movement, Lexx was having another nightmare. She'd had them every night since their zombie invasion. Her body twitched slightly from whatever monster was chasing her this time. A soft groan was heard. Lexx again twitched but didn't wake. Brandon's hand slowly moved across her back. Lexx gasped and jumped away from him. Brandon looked at her and smiled gently.

"You were having a nightmare," he said in a weak sounding voice.

Lexx stared at Brandon and his familiar smile. It melted her heart. She hugged him and sobbed softly on his shoulder. He gently held her against him and laughed.

"I'm happy to see you too."

Lexx pulled away and wiped her tears. He seemed weak but pretty much his usual self. "I've been worried sick about you since the car accident."

"Car accident?" he asked gently with surprise. "Is that what happened?"

"You don't remember?" she asked with surprise as she stared at him.

She didn't know why she was surprised. Most coma patients needed time for their brains to catch up and blocking traumatic events was very common.

He considered her question and uncertainly shook his head. "I remember we'd picked up that kid at the morgue." His look conveyed his confusion. "Nothing after that though. I'm pretty sure it was raining." He studied her a moment then smiled warmly. "What did I miss?"

Lexx stared at Brandon, pondered over how to respond, and then forced a smile. "Not much."

"Oh," he replied then considered something and sank into thought. He tilted his head and stared at her with a curious look.

"Are you sure? I swear I remember hearing something about you having a date."

She stared into his brown eyes with surprise then smiled and laughed. It was good having him back. Lexx then hesitated and stared into his brown eyes a moment longer. She found that curious. She could have sworn his eyes were green.

The End

Other books by Holly Copella!
Reviews left on Amazon are appreciated!

"The Battle for Andrea Maria"

A cruise ship attack turns six survivors into overnight celebrities after they take credit for the heroic act of a stowaway who died saving them.

The cruise is just what Jess needed--a bit of harmless fun far from her daily grind. But what begins as a relaxing vacation turns into a desperate fight for her life when terrorists take over the ship and start piling up bodies. Teaming up with a mysterious stowaway, Jess attempts to send out a distress call but knows they cannot wait for help to come. If she or the few remaining passengers have any hope for survival, Jess must act now. The papers dub it "The Battle for *Andrea Maria*," but to Jess it is the moment she fought side-by-side with her enigmatic Romeo, saving the ship--and losing him. She thinks the story ends there, but really, the nightmare is just beginning...

"Insanely Deadly"

When the dead return to life, it's up to an admiral's daughter and a mildly insane, former war hero to save their small town.

Jetta Cross, a Navy Admiral's daughter, is tasked with keeping her father's comrade, a former war hero turned town crazy, grounded in the real world. Capt. John Hunter is still fighting the war in his head, where imaginary dead people are part of his world. When a viral outbreak brings about a zombie uprising, Hunter is left to his own devices. He must resume his role as a one-man commando unit in order to destroy the ravenous undead. With Hunter still fighting his own inner demons as well as the undead, the townspeople fear their zombie neighbors may not be the only threat. Stranded at the island's luxurious resort with a handful of workers, Jetta is forced to live up to her father's reputation and take charge of the deteriorating situation at the hotel. She must wage her own war against the infected before the government declares her hometown a total loss.

"Deadly Institution"

A town recluse suspected of killing his wife teams up with a young woman in order to stop a killer.

After being accused of murdering his wife, Konrad Asher turns his back on the town that once adored him. Ten years later, he still holds his grudge and the title of the most feared man in town. With the reopening of the burned mental institution, where his wife had died, former employees are now murdered one-by-one, throwing suspicion back on Asher. A young local reporter, Jacey, is forced to reveal her long-time friendship with the infamous recluse in order to clear his name not only in the recent murders but to exonerate him in the death of his wife as well. Will Jacey's relationship with Asher invite the killer closer to her? Or is the killer already in her life?

"Screenplays: The Island Collection"
"Jungle Princess", "A.L.F. Resort", "Brighton Island"

Discover how romance and fun in the sun can be downright *chilling*!

"Jungle Princess" is a romantic/thriller that leaves a teenage girl stranded on an island with two male shipmates and a creature of "unknown" origin. She soon discovers the island is home to an abandoned prison with several prisoners roaming free. What really killed over one hundred prisoners? And is it still out there--?

"A.L.F. Resort" is a romantic/thriller set on an island resort with Artificial Life Forms as the main draw. At this resort, all your fantasies come true...until a malfunction removes safety inhibitors on the A.L.F.'s. Zombies, biker gangs, and mobsters run amuck, turning fantasies into nightmares. A young reporter gets more of a story than she anticipates, but will she survive long enough to write the story?

"Brighton Island" is a romantic/thriller set on a private island. When the owner's niece brings her psychic friend to the mansion, his presence awakens the spirits' tortured souls. As the psychic attempts to solve the old murders, the niece is confronted with the possibility that she's next to join the mansion ghosts. Stranded on the island with a crazed killer, her uncle wages his own war to save them. Will his "shock and awe" tactics actually save them or get them killed?

"Reaper of Souls" A fantasy short story

A young woman must outwit an evil sorcerer in order to save her brother or become one of his minions forever.

Unwilling to believe her brother is dead, Reggie discovers an underhanded deal made with Kahn, a less than ethical sorcerer, who collects humans to serve as slaves in his kingdom. In order to rescue her brother from his horrible fate, she must complete his failed task or be forced to serve Kahn forever. After being transported to his world, Reggie realizes that even if she beats Kahn at his own game, she's at his mercy for him to uphold his end of the deal. All seems lost until Kahn's discontented, self-serving brother, Helsing, arrives. Can Reggie convince Helsing to help her? And at what cost?

"Town Darling"

After surviving a brutal attack that claims the lives of those she loves, a young woman seeks revenge on a corrupt town.

Going back home is never easy, but for Casey, it means returning to her corrupt hometown where she barely survived a brutal attack. Accompanied by two *family friends*, she seeks justice for the night that destroyed her life. Her physical scars are nothing compared to her emotional ones, forcing the local sheriff to believe that the town darling is back for revenge. As the conspiracy for her revenge appears to be leading up to the coveted town fair, the sheriff is determined to stop her from fulfilling her vengeful scheme...but guilt over his role on that fateful night continues to haunt him. His desperate need for Casey's forgiveness could be his undoing.

"Dead Village"

After strange happenings isolate a small resort town from the rest of the world, nearly one hundred residents seek refuge at the closed hotel. Only eight survive the night. And that's just the beginning...

One day after the entire population of Fox Ridge Village disappears, a car wreck forces several unsuspecting crash victims to seek help at the closed summer hotel. Within the hotel, they discover the grisly aftermath of a brutal slaughter. Crash victims Vander and Devon, a reluctant clairvoyant, team up to solve the riddle of the "haunted hotel" and the mass hysteria plaguing the remaining survivors. By the time they discover the hotel's secret, they're already drawn into the hysteria. As the body count continues to climb, it's a race to isolate the source and bring everyone back to reality before they kill one another. Will Devon be able to communicate with the traumatized spirits before their fate becomes her own?

"Death Displacement"

A grief-stricken man travels back in time to seek revenge on the woman who murdered his girlfriend but inadvertently falls in love with her.

Kane is about to marry the woman he loves. His life is perfect. A few weeks before the wedding, a vindictive woman from his girlfriend's past mysteriously arrives and kills her. He learns of a traumatic accident that happened five years earlier, which triggers Riley's hatred for his girlfriend. Distraught over his girlfriend's death, Kane uses an antique time machine to travel into the past in order to find and destroy the woman responsible. When he runs into Riley's younger self, he realizes she's not the monster she later becomes, and he can't bring himself to destroy her. With a little help from his oddball friend from the past, they formulate a plan to prevent the accident that sends Riley down her destructive path. Kane's plan backfires when he falls for the younger Riley. His new tortured existence is further complicated when future Riley, his girlfriend's killer, shows up with her own devious agenda that doesn't include him. Will he be able to stop the time ripple, which ultimately ends with his girlfriend's death? Or will future Riley take him out of the timeline forever--

Coming Soon!
"Witness Protection"

After witnessing an execution, a resourceful young woman attempts to disappear while being pursued by a hitman and a handsome federal agent.

Helicopter pilot, Jackie Remus, reluctantly agrees to go on a date with the governor. Her date is cut short when she witnesses the governor's hitman killing a federal agent. After narrowly escaping the date with her life, she is placed into protective custody with U.S. Marshals. When the safe house is breached and the Marshals are killed, Jackie makes a daring escape from both the hired killers and the handsome FBI agent, who wants to place her back into protective custody. With a little help from her sly and crafty friend, Monroe, she's convinced she can disappear until the trial. While on her journey to meet with her friend, she solicits help from a few shady but lovable characters along the way. Although she manages to stay one-step ahead of the governor's hitman, Agent Falcone remains in hot pursuit. Will Jackie reach Monroe before she's captured and returned to protective custody? Or will the hitman get to her first?

ABOUT THE AUTHOR

Holly Copella has been writing since the age of twelve when her frustration at a book's poor plot drove her to author her own story. Over the last decade, she's written a number of screenplays, some of which she's now adapting into novels. Her fascination with zombies and other darker material lends an edge to her writing, which tends to lean toward horror. As a fan of Agatha Christie, she appreciates the craft of a good plot and the importance of creating significant characters.

Hailing from Pennsylvania, Copella lives in the Endless Mountains on a farm with her rescue horses and other animals. In addition to writing and reading fiction, she enjoys riding horses and traveling to Las Vegas and Disney World.